Vegas

By Matthew Lee

BunnyLovesBigCarrots@gmail.com

A blazing hot Vegas Saturday afternoon and I'm at the mall with my wife Julie instead of home watching Alabama crush Auburn. Whatever. The one redeeming point of this shopping trip is I know it will include a stop at Victoria's Secret where I will join Julie in the dressing room as she tries to find a swimsuit to fit her outrageous body. I ran my eyes over my wife and remembered her naked.

At the moment, she wore a clingy, red, short-sleeved top that showed off just a little of her impressive cleavage, and tight black shorts that hid her bubble butt. I hated those shorts. The black was so dark it was difficult to see just how fit she was. Her long, dark brown hair was pulled back into an efficient pony-tail. When Julie shops, she's all business.

Forty-five minutes later we enter Victoria's Secret. A pretty Asian salesgirl approaches us, immediately asking if we'd like to sample a new lotion. Julie sticks her hands out. I wave the girl off and wander away as Julie and the salesgirl, who introduces herself as Gina, begin earnestly discussing the wonderful merits of this fine new Victoria's Secret product.

"David?" my wife asks. "Where are you going?"

Damn. Caught.

"I was going to find something I'd like to see you in and get it for you."

Julie and Gina exchanged knowing grins and my wife tells me to go ahead. I step up to her and lean down to kiss her forehead. I slip away.

Victoria's Secret in Las Vegas is not like Victoria's Secret stores in other states. The number of hot young girls in this town is ridiculous. I browsed the store and everywhere I went, nubile girls, either customers or employees, crawled over the store like ants. I drank them all in while keeping an eye out for Julie. She hates it when I look at other girls.

Soon my wandering took me towards the back of the store. I was looking at a black teddy for Jules when I focused beyond it and realized I had the perfect angle on the dressing rooms. As I watched, a door opened and a salesgirl handed an outfit inside to a gorgeous redhead no more than eighteen and nude from the waist up. Her pale breasts were large and topped with bright pink nipples. I acted like I was looking at the item in hand but really I devoured that lovely young thing. When she saw me, she didn't react at all. Either she believed I was focused on the top in my hand or she just didn't give a shit I was viewing her topless.

When the salesgirl left, the redhead stepped back inside but left her door opened enough for me to see. She turned her back and I took advantage. I lowered the top and just stared at her reflection in the dressing room mirror. This girl was smoking hot. When she slipped off her shorts and exposed her neatly trimmed pussy, a surge of blood filled my dick. I gawked as long as I could without getting caught, and then realized too late the redhead watched me the whole time by bouncing her gaze off other mirrors. I found myself looking her directly in the eye.

I expected her to call me a creep or slam her dressing room door but she didn't. Instead, she smiled and faced me, ran her fingers through her long beautiful hair, and slowly shut her door ending the show.

I got the hell away from there. I found Julie with an armful of clothing and handed her the item I'd found for her.

"You okay?" she asked.

"Yes, but getting hungry."

"Me too. Let's finish and grab a bite."

In the dressing room, Julie stripped and began trying on items. One was too small across her chest and she asked me to go find a larger size. As I left her room and shut the door,

Redhead was just exiting her room. She gave me a big smile and I returned it, falling into step behind her and loving her great ass. When she turned for the register I turned to find Julie a larger size. What a great day.

I found the top and headed back. As I drew close, I noticed an older man standing at a rack, pretending to examine an item just like I'd done earlier. I chuckled. I guess all men are dogs. I took an angle that allowed me to see where he was looking and was shocked to discover he was ogling Julie! Had I not latched the door properly? I was angry and took a step towards him, planning on publicly shaming him and getting in his face. He was taller and heavier than me but what could he do in a public place?

My third step brought me to a halt.

Julie knew he was watching!

Bouncing her reflection off various mirrors, I saw her smile at him. She was topless like Redhead had been and acting innocent, but I saw in her eyes that she was aware of her voyeur. I leaned into a display of bathrobes and watched her flirt.

He was mesmerized. Although Julie's breasts have swelled to much more than I can fit in my hand, her nipples are still puffy. He was staring a hole right through my wife. Her recent growth spurt hasn't affected the firmness of her tits so while big, they do not hang at all. Some of her girlfriends asked if she had them done and Julie loves it every time they do.

She took her time closing her door. I waited for her new fan to walk away and then I entered her room again and handed her the top. I thought about telling her what I'd seen her do but didn't for two reasons; first, I'm a hypocrite, and second, while watching, I quickly found my initial anger replaced by arousal. I liked that another guy saw her. I liked that Julie wanted to show herself off. My reaction surprised me but I guess we never know how we'll react to something until actually confronted by it.

I'm not merely the only person she's ever had sex with; I'm the only guy who has shown her any attention at all. Julie grew up an ugly, skinny, nerdy, socially-awkward girl and has only blossomed within the last year, especially the last six months. We've been together three years. She's highly intelligent, independent, and has a quirky sense of humor I love. I met her at school and we hit it off but she thought I wanted her as a friend. Guys always wanted her as just a friend. When I tried to kiss her the first time she freaked out and pushed me away, and then immediately jumped on me and kissed me.

She's on the school swim team and works out all the time but could not put on any weight until one magical day hormones kicked in and they haven't stopped. Her body now is amazing.

An hour later we left with two big bags of new things and even deeper in debt. Julie was excited to have them and I was excited to see her wear them.

The voyeur got me thinking and I resolved to pay more attention to the people around us. My suspicions were rapidly confirmed; Julie turned heads wherever we went. I don't know how I'd missed it before but I had and in a big way. Pride swelled that I'd landed such a desirable woman. I had a bounce in my step. My chest puffed.

After lunch it was time to shop for me. We entered a men's clothier and Julie insisted I try on several suits. I recently started a new job which required them and I currently cycled through the same three. We found a dressing room and it was my turn. Julie brought me different shirts to try with the suits.

When she left to find me the right shade of green, she didn't come back. I finished the shirts I had and waited for a while and then I went looking for her, but couldn't find her. The store was virtually deserted with the lone salesman helping an older couple. I decided to return to my dressing room and wait and on my way back I noticed and archway that led to another small area where they kept all the clearance items.

As I rounded a display of sports coats, I saw her. She was talking to the older guy she'd flashed in Victoria's Secret! He must have followed us after we left. She held two green shirts in her hand. He held two blue in his. I couldn't hear their conversation. Julie was smiling and laughing at everything he said and he was gazing at her intensely as he spoke. My first instinct was to barge in and disrupt them.

But I didn't.

For the second time that day I allowed this man to enjoy a moment of my wife. I don't know why I stopped, but I did. I wanted to watch her in this situation. I wanted to see what would happen next.

He pointed to the shirts she held and raised his own and I saw Julie listen and then nod her head and glance at her watch. With Julie following, Older Man walked to some dressing rooms and stepped inside one. He pulled the door mostly closed but not all the way. Julie stood to the side so she couldn't see in but after a moment began to shuffle her feet until she could. I moved behind a rack of sale shirts so I had the same view as she.

Older Man peeled off his shirt, exposing his hairy chest. His muscles were much bigger than mine. If he noticed Julie watching, he hid it. He kicked off his shoes. I wondered why he needed to take off his shoes if he was only trying on shirts when down came his pants.

His penis was huge and his shaved balls were gigantic. My penis is a little bigger than average and I am not shy changing at the gym or visiting the doctor. I've only had intercourse with Julie but I did receive a few hand jobs growing up and all of those girls commented how nice and big I was. This guy was more than me by a lot, and he was still soft.

Julie saw it and her hands came up to her face. She turned bright red and stepped back where she could no longer see into his dressing room. A minute later Older Man stepped out wearing a new shirt and pants. The pants must have already been in the dressing room. He asked my wife her opinion. A clearly flustered Julie made a few comments and Older Man disappeared into the dressing room again and then moments later stepped out wearing the other shirt. Julie again advised him and he entered the room once more.

My wife slid a little to the right in order to see in just as Older Man began swapping his new pants for old. This time Julie stood her ground and it turned me on that she wanted to see it again. He wore no underwear so his dick and balls bumped and flopped as he dressed. He tucked everything down a pant leg and re-buckled his belt. At the last second, Julie quickly turned away to avoid getting caught but I saw his face; he knew she'd watched.

Older Man emerged and they spoke briefly, and then he shook her hand and gave her a business card and left for the register. I hurried back to my dressing room and Julie joined me. I said nothing. I tried on a few more clothes, including the two green shirts she held, and we made our selections and checked out. Twenty minutes later we were back at our apartment. We dropped our bags on the bedroom floor.

My wife said she needed a shower and I opened us both a beer. I was relieved she wanted to bathe because I needed some time alone to think.

My reactions earlier surprised and confused me and I wanted to sort them out. I understood getting angry but why didn't I stay angry? Why hadn't I confronted her and him? Why did I get excited when she wanted to see his penis a second time? Shouldn't I have been jealous?

I sipped my beer. I enjoyed him looking at her and her looking at him. Every friend I have would have lost their minds in that situation. I knew I was a visual guy but was I really this visual?

I heard the shower come on.

Should I say something to Julie? What was the harm, really? I know she loved all this new attention and after a lifetime of rejection and taunting from her peers, I wanted her to have it. I decided to keep my mouth shut.

After a while the shower stopped. I was reaching for the television remote when movement from the hallway caught my eye. I turned.

Julie wore a cherry-red lace teddy with matching underwear. Her big tits looked spectacular. Through the lace of her panties I was just able to make out the light brown and neatly trimmed fur on her pussy.

"I am taking you shopping more often," I croaked.

She giggled and jumped onto my lap, kissing me.

Twenty minutes later I pulled out, as always, shooting my load on her leg, and we tumbled to the floor, sweaty and exhausted and gasping for breath. After we'd laid a while calmed. Julie spoke.

"How big are you, Baby?"

"What? What do you mean? My penis?" I asked, shocked.

She held it up by the head. It was soft now and trying to nap.

"Yeah, like, how long and how big around? Have you ever measured?"

"No," I lied.

"Let's measure."

"You have to give me a minute Honey. I just came. If you want to measure I need to be hard."

"Okay. Tell me when."

What the hell? We cuddled with her head on my chest. I knew she was looking down at my dick because I occasionally felt her eyelashes blinking against my skin.

"I'm curious why you want to know, Honey." I said. "What does it matter?"

"The only real live penis I've ever seen is yours, Baby. Girls wonders about such things."

"Mine's a little above average."

She reached down to play with it again.

"I'm glad. That makes me feel lucky. I've seen dicks online. Little ones look cute but they turn me off. Big ones look sexy but it's hard to tell how big they really are or if they're even real. I like the bigger ones much better. I like yours; I just can't tell how it would compare to some of the ones I've seen."

A question occurred to me but I hesitated to ask it out of fear for the answer. Finally I asked it anyway.

"I'm glad you like it. Would you like it more if it were bigger? Like, if I walked around the apartment naked and my penis was bigger, would that make you want sex more?"

She laughed out loud. "Yes! Of course, silly. When they were small you always wished my boobs were bigger. I did too. Don't bigger boobs turn you on more than smaller ones?"

She was right. "Yeah, I guess so. Oh well, looks like we're stuck with each other."

She rolled onto her back and looked down at her tits. She cupped them both and pulled them towards her face, studying them.

"That's not fair; my boobs keep growing. They're way bigger than they were last year and it looks like they plan on growing even bigger, but your penis is the same size. You get to enjoy variety while I'm stuck with exactly the same thing every time."

Now it was my turn to laugh.

"Lucky me!"

I rolled over on top of her and sucked a puffy nipple into my mouth.

"I'm serious, David."

I let her nipple pop out. "What do you want me to do about it, Honey? Your boobs are bigger but they are still your boobs, I'm still having sex with the same person. I can't make my penis bigger. For you to experience a bigger penis I'd have to let you have sex with someone else." I laughed again, this time at that preposterous idea. I expected her to laugh too, but she didn't. Instead she gave me a serious look and waited. I decided to wait her out, but I didn't last long.

"What?" I asked, exasperated. "What are you thinking?"

"We got married so young," she said.

"What's that supposed to mean?" I rolled off and onto my back, a gallon of adrenaline suddenly racing through my body. She snuggled up to me again, her head on my chest.

"David, I love you, I will always love you. You saw me and loved me when nobody else did and I'll never forget that and never leave you. You are my best friend. But let's be honest with each other: don't you look at other girls sometimes and wonder what it would be like? Don't answer; I don't want to hear it. I'm just saying I worry we married too soon and our decision will come back to haunt us. We've only had sex with each other. Are we missing out? Aren't you worried we'll get bored? Forever is such a long time."

I knew what was really happening; Julie, my little ugly-duckling, had grown into a swan and discovered she loved all the attention she'd been missing. Her options had increased dramatically and she wondered what she was worth on the open market. I was hurt and intimidated frightened. I considered mentioning her dressing room antics but held off.

"I'm confused," I stated. "It sounds like you wish you could have sex with others but still have your relationship with me?"

She pondered my question, which sucked.

"Yes," she sighed. "No. Not exactly. I know relationships don't work like that. It's confusing. I definitely want to stay with you; I'm just worried about us. I'm curious. Don't you wonder about others?"

I ignored her question. "You've thought a lot about this."

"I have. It's been on my mind for months. Your comment earlier about a new lover for me made me think of it again so I said something. Sorry. I should have kept my mouth shut. This is too difficult a subject for a couple to talk about. It automatically sounds like I'm thinking of leaving you. I'm not. Not at all. I swear."

"No Baby, you should be able to tell me anything. You're my best friend too. I want to know whatever you're thinking and feeling, no matter what. We'll handle it together."

She hugged me and squeezed hard.

"I don't have an answer for you right now," I continued. "That's a lot all at once. I promise to think about what you said, okay? I admit I like it when guys check you out so maybe we can play a little game where you get to flirt and enjoy all this new attention?"

"Really? You won't get jealous or angry? You'll let me have some fun?"

I nodded.

"You're the best," she said. "You're amazing. I love you, David."

"I love you, Julie."

I decided to go for it. "You know, I saw you today, in the dressing room. You and that older man." Her face turned away and I felt her body tense. "First at Victoria's Secret, when you showed off for him and then after, when he showed off for you. I just happened to catch both. I'm wondering if those events have something to do with how you're feeling about us right now. Do they?"

She turned her blushing face to mine.

"Yes, I have to admit they do."

"Tell me."

She collected her thoughts a minute before responding, checking my expression to determine how much she should admit.

"I loved the way he looked at me," she began. "No man has ever looked at me with such desire in his eyes, not even you, David. His eyes *burned* with want. He was like an animal. Honestly, his attention made my legs weak. I loved showing him my new body. Later, while you were trying on clothes, he approached me to ask my opinion about some shirts and pants he wanted. I suspected it was all bullshit, like he just wanted an excuse to check me out, but I played along to see what he was up to. He's older, but he's really hot, Honey. He's so good-looking."

"Go on, tell me more."

"I don't want to hurt your feelings."

"I can take it. Tell me the truth. That's what we're doing here."

"When he took his shirt off I got tingly all over. He's so sexy. His body is amazing. Then he took off his pants and I saw his, thing, and I got turned on. Did you see it? He's really big. Way bigger than you, and you're not small. I was surprised it mattered how big he was, but it did. I was shocked how much it mattered. I wondered what it would be like, you know, to be with him. What would one that big feel like? Your penis feels much better than your finger because it's much larger. Would his penis feel better than yours for the same reason?"

I can't tell you why, but hearing her talk like this made my dick grow. She noticed. She kept her gaze on my shifting penis as she continued.

"I wanted to touch it, Honey. I didn't, but you said tell the truth so I confess I wanted to. Did you see it? It was beautiful; so masculine and strong, so thick and long. Most of my girlfriends think dicks are ugly, but I don't."

"I'm glad you didn't touch his dick," I managed to say.

She reached down and took my penis in her hand and squeezed.

"I wondered how his dick would look hard. How big would it get? Just imagining turned me on so much. I was surprised by how badly I wanted to put it in my mouth. I had to look away."

Blood surged into my dick. I'd been growing harder as she talked and I suspected she was laying it on thick to test my reaction. Now I was hard as a rock. Julie lowered her mouth to my penis, enveloping me in a hot, wet slide. I moaned. She sucked hard and bobbed a few times, then jumped up. I groaned with frustration. Julie never swallows my load, instead pulling off and finishing me with her hand, but I still hope every time that this will be the time.

"Hang on," she insisted. She ran to the cabinet and returned with a tape measure. "Six and a half long, five inches around. I'll have to look that up and let you know, but for now stay there."

She climbed on top of me and settled her wet and tight young pussy around my shaft. Before I could do anything my wife started fucking me hard. I rested my hands on her hips but there was nothing for me to do. She was using me and my hard dick to get off and I liked it.

Her head was back and her eyes were closed and her long hair was tickling my thighs and I wondered if she was imagining me inside her or if Older Man was fucking her right now. My gut told me Older Man and again, I didn't get angry, I got harder.

She cupped both big and ridiculously firm tits and pinched her nipples. She lifted a tit to her mouth and sucked a nipple. I got so turned on listening to her orgasm I came too, throwing her off of me and pulling out just in time, spraying my stomach and chest.

This time we both showered. Neither of us brought the subject up again. We both had plenty to think about. Later that evening we were in bed watching a movie when something occurred to me.

"Jules?" I asked. "Did I see that man hand you something? Like a business card?"

The popcorn stopped half-way to her mouth.

"Yes."

"May I see it?"

"Okay." She leaned over the side of the bed and fished through her purse. She handed me the card. It read: *Jacob Brighton Photography* with a number and an email. The back was blank.

"What did he say when he handed it to you?" I asked.

She seemed embarrassed. "That I should be modeling bikinis and underwear and making tons of money. I said I wasn't tall enough for modeling and he said that was true, but I could make a lot of money modeling swimsuits or undergarments or lingerie. He asked my age and if I'd any experience. He told me to call him but I said I had to talk it over with you."

"Why didn't you?"

"After thinking about it I decided not to. Those girls are gorgeous. I'm not pretty enough or sexy enough. People would laugh. He was just hitting on me."

I was dumbstruck. My jaw hit the bed.

"Are you crazy, Jules? You are stunning! You are super-hot! I'm not telling you to do it, I'm just saying you totally could."

Julie blushed again. She tried to snatch the card from me but I was too quick.

"Really?" she asked. "You really think so? We could sure use the extra money. Should I try it, Baby?"

"Use your awesome Internet research skills and find out if he's legit and if he is, try it and see if you like it. At least get a bunch of questions together and call and talk with him."

Julie was beaming. She jumped out of bed and stood before the full-length mirror, turning side to side, scrutinizing her body. She peeled her nightshirt off and repeated the process nude.

"Oh Baby, are you sure?" she asked, insecurities running wild.

"Julie, I swear to you, I know you can't see it but you have a world-class body. Your face is gorgeous. Your hair, your skin, your eyes, your smile; everyone notices you."

She wanted so badly to believe me.

"Okay!" she exclaimed, "I'll check him out."

She turned on the computer and soon the glow of the monitor filled the room. A nagging anxiety settled into the pit of my stomach. Was I doing something stupid here?

***

Three weeks later we sat in the large waiting room at Jacob Brighton Photography surrounded by fake plants and shag carpet. Four doors led from the room. The setting sun glared in the only window. On the coffee table along with old magazines was Jacob's portfolio book and it was impressive. At the front of the book were all the generic ads for soup and kid's clothes and toothpaste, but as we turned the pages we discovered swimsuit and intimate-wear models. Julie glanced through the beachwear but really studied the women dressed in lingerie.

Julie insisted I accompany her today and Jacob easily agreed. If she made even half the money he said she would, we'd get both credit cards paid off in less than a year, and those have been hanging around our necks for a long time.

Ten minutes later the black studio door opened and Jacob walked out with a drop-dead gorgeous blue-eyed blonde. Julie took one look at that girl and her self-confidence and enthusiasm imploded. I saw fear rise in her eyes. I took Julie's hands in mine.

"Don't worry about her," I whispered as Jacob and Blondie said their good-byes. "You are prettier than her and you have a much better body. Look at her, Jules. You are in much better shape than she is."

I wasn't just saying it. Blondie was tall with big boobs but her skin was lightly dimpled from fat and her face wasn't as pretty as Julie's. Julie looked her up and down and I saw some confidence return. She met my eyes and nodded.

"I'm okay," she murmured.

Jacob shut the big outer door behind Blondie and turned to us. We made formal introductions all around and he welcomed me but said for insurance reasons, I would not be allowed into the studio. I said I understood. Julie brought along all her swimsuits in a bag but he said he wouldn't need them. His clients wanted to see photos of the model wearing their suits. Julie left her suits with me and entered the studio. The door closed with a click.

I returned to flipping through the portfolio book. The deeper I went, the less the models wore. The last two pages were especially hot as the girls were virtually nude. Jacob used lighting and shadow to incredible effect and this actually heightened the sexuality of the pictures. He had serious talent. I closed the back cover and flipped the book face up. In the bottom right corner I noticed a small sticker with "1 of 2" hand written in black ink. So there was a second book somewhere?

I looked around the waiting room but saw nothing. I knew the big door led outside to the parking lot and the black door led to the studio, but where did the other two doors lead? I checked one and it opened into a restroom. I checked the other and although the knob was locked, the door wasn't shut fully so it swung open. I gazed into Jacob's office.

I stepped quickly to the studio door and placed my ear against it. I heard muffled voices a fair distance away so I decided to risk it. Four big steps brought me inside his office.

I glanced rapidly at the shelves along the wall and then scanned his desk top. Nothing. I opened the large cabinet doors next to his desk and was greeted by six large monitors, three of which were clearly recording what was happening inside the studio, three that were dark.

On the first monitor I saw Julie wearing a small black bikini and holding a beach ball above her head while Jacob snapped pictures. The second monitor was a distance shot that captured the entire studio; Jacob and Julie and the backdrop and all his equipment and lights. The third camera was pointed behind a free standing screen. There was no sound.

As I watched, Julie lowered the ball and stepped behind the screen to change into the next bikini. She disappeared from two monitors and appeared on the third.

I saw everything as she untied her top and bottoms. Jacob was busy ignoring her and changing lens and background but why try to catch a glimpse when you are recording everything in close-up detail? I got angry. He'd already recorded my wife nude!

Jacob lifted his head and he must have said something to Julie because her head came up too and I saw her lips move. Jacob stepped to a small door in the studio wall and opened it, flipping on a light. When he did, the other three monitors came to life.

This was a storage room which contained extra equipment and supplies and scenery but what caught my eye and was the focal point for the three remaining cameras was a large king-sized bed against the left wall. Pervert Mother Fucker!

Julie finished slipping into the next suit; a red one-piece cut low under her arms exposing plenty of side-boob. She looked hot. I reminded myself I was angry. She exited that screen and I picked her up on the other two. Jacob returned.

I noticed Jacob had a large light blocking the door to the waiting room so I knew I would have time if he headed back. He'd have to move that light first. I continued scanning the shelves and soon found the second portfolio book. I flipped open the first page.

A young, hot, and wildly sexy brunette girl stared back at me. She wore a see-through bathrobe and gazed right into the camera. I turned the page. Her tits were small but her ass was perfect. She obviously worked-out. Two pages later she spread her pussy for the camera and three pages after that her tongue wrapped around the large head of what I was certain was Jacob's cock. I got a kick in the guts as I remembered Julie telling me when she'd first seen it she wanted it in her mouth. Apparently this girl felt the same way.

I checked the monitors briefly and Julie still wore the red one-piece but the backdrop had changed from a pool to a tropical beach.

I turned pages. The brunette gave way to a redhead and then several blonde girls. There were pictures of every one of them sucking Jacob's big dick. When I realized the pictures were taken on the bed in the storage room, I knew that meant Jacob also possessed video of each encounter, and I bet they didn't end with just a blowjob. I only saw those pictures because at that point Jacob still held the camera. The video would capture everything that happened after he set the camera down.

I glanced at the monitor and Julie was changing again, this time into a tiny green suit that was little more than three triangles of thin fabric. Her tits spilled out all the way around including underneath and the material barely covered her puffy nipples. She adjusted it carefully. Her pussy was covered but a little soft hair peeked out at the top and no amount of adjusting could hide it. A string disappeared between her firm butt cheeks.

I wanted to hate this guy. I really did. But what a set-up! Jacob was a genius. He'd prowl the malls for innocent new talent, bring them back with promises of wealth, film them almost nude and score fairly often with incredibly hot young girls. Jacob was the man. I'd make sure Julie never saw him again.

I skipped to the back pages of the book. This was the hardcore stuff. I recognized the brunette again but now three well-endowed guys fucked her at the same time and one of them was black! Her eyes looked drunk or drugged and I wondered if Jacob got them wasted first. I studied her face more closely and admitted she seemed to be present and enjoying herself.

I needed to collect Julie and get out of there. I put everything back exactly the way it was and watched them on the screen, keeping an eye that nothing happened and returning to the waiting room only when I saw them wrapping up.

I was flipping through *People* magazine when they entered. I rose, shook Jacob's hand and asked Julie how it went. She said she was nervous at first but Jacob made her feel beautiful and sexy and she quickly relaxed.

"You were amazing," he stated. "Easily the most gorgeous girl I've ever worked with, and now here's the best part!" Jacob handed Julie a stack of cash. "You have my number," he continued. "Let me know when you want more work. I'm afraid I have to rush and get ready for my next appointment."

We all shook hands again and Julie and I left. I noticed Julie looked at him with wonder in her eyes. My wife seemed to be smitten. I thought no more about it, but I should have.

On the ride home I told her everything I'd uncovered. Julie was shocked. I told her I did not want her going back there, fully expecting her to quickly agree.

She hesitated. "Why?" she asked.

Now it was my turn to be shocked.

"Because he's a predator, Julie! Because you're not safe around him! He gives girls drugs or alcohol and plays on their dreams and then fucks them and records it. Are you kidding me?"

"But now I know it, Sweetheart. Thanks to your detective work we're onto his game. Look how much I got paid, Baby! For just two hours! I will be on guard for his tricks and I won't drink anything he gives me. He doesn't fuck every girl he photographs. Maybe he only fucks the girls that want him to. I'll be one of the ones that get away."

I didn't like her plan and told her so. She countered and assured me she'd be fine. We drove in silence for a while. I wanted to order her to never return. I wanted to forbid her. I knew my reaction was immature but I was powerless to control it.

Julie turned to face me, grinning. "So, in those pictures, you saw it hard. How did it look? When he's erect is he really big like I thought he would be?"

My jaw fell open. I could not believe she was asking me that. I ignored her.

"I bet it is," she went on, looking out the windshield. "I bet it's fucking huge and beautiful and manly and frightening. I can picture it so easily."

She was trying to goad me but I was in no mood to play. I changed the subject. "Tell me what modeling was like. You said you were nervous at first. How did you relax? Was it fun?"

"It was awesome, Honey. I was scared at first, and felt like I wasn't pretty enough. Jacob knew exactly what I was thinking and reassured me. As we took pictures he said really sweet and flattering things. He complimented my body and my face. He said I photograph well. He was very convincing. After a while I started to feel sexy and got into it. Before I knew it I was turned on. David, I might be an exhibitionist. I never knew that about myself. That's another reason I want to keep going; I really liked showing off. Don't worry, everything will be fine."

I wanted to believe her but my gut told me otherwise.

"I have a very bad feeling about all this," I told her. "I really want you to stay away from him. I can't come with you every time, Honey."

"David, I'm a big girl. I promise if I ever feel like I need to leave, I will."

I pouted the rest of the way home.

Julie showered and came out of the bathroom wearing a towel. I was about to ask her if she was hungry but the look in her eyes stopped me. She let the towel fall to the ground.

If I am married to her for a thousand years I'll never get over how sexy she is. In addition to the body and the face, there is an aura of sweet innocence about her that a woman this physically attractive should not have. I am drawn in and captivated before I catch myself. She has no idea how stunning she's become.

I crossed the room and crushed her with kisses and felt her melt under my hands. I roughly squeezed her large breasts and pinched her nipples, causing her to moan from deep in her chest. I spun her around and smacked her ass and then I remembered her defiance and refusal to stop the modeling and I smacked her again, much harder, fueled by my irritation with her. She yelped but did not move away, awaiting the next slap. I gave it to her, harder than the other two and she cried out. When I touched her pussy she was soaked.

I spun her to face me. Raw, barely contained passion filled her eyes. She was desperately horny, longing to be taken. Her naked lust frightened me a little. I was shocked by it. I'd never seen that look in her eyes before.

Before I was able to make my next move, she dropped to her knees with a frustrated whimper and fumbled to free my dick. The moment she saw it she inhaled me down to my balls, choking and gagging and forcing every inch into her mouth and down her throat. I held her head and short-fucked her mouth. She sensed how fast I would orgasm and slipped me out trying to slow things down but before I could stop myself I blasted a hot load straight into open air. I heard her cry, "Noooo!" before my legs went weak and I fell onto the love seat.

Julie let out a frustrated groan and curled into a ball on the floor, fucking herself on her fingers. I felt bad for cumming so fast so I dropped to my knees and began licking her, but somehow that seemed to make things worse. I used my fingers on her and my tongue too but the squirming and writhing and distressed moans and gasps told me I was failing.

"What, Baby," I asked, annoyed. "What do you want me to do?"

She grabbed a handful of my hair and twisted my face up to hers.

"Fuck me!" she yelled. "I need to be fucked! Pound me, Baby. I desperately want a hard cock inside me. I *need* a hard cock inside me. A big one. A big hard cock buried in my cunt!"

I'd never seen her act this horny.

"Well I can't, Honey. I'll need some time first. Let me get you off with my mouth."

She drew in a bushel of air and let it out in a long sigh. She pulled her legs up to her chest assuming a fetal position.

"No, it's okay, I'm sorry for yelling, David. Just hold me."

I spooned her and neither of us spoke a long time.

"I'm sorry I came so fast, Honey," I finally offered.

"No, don't feel badly about it. I'm actually flattered. You looked at me with such lust in your eyes. I loved it. Let's dress up and go out. I need to burn some energy."

I was ready quickly and then waited for her. It was worth the wait. From the back of the apartment I heard her ask, "How do I look?"

She came out of our bedroom wearing a little black dress that was painted on. The dress plunged in the back all the way to the dimples above her butt and plunged in the front almost to her belly button. She obviously wore no bra. The tight dress was short; easily the shortest thing I'd ever seen her wear, with a hem much closer to her pussy than her knees. The sleeves came down to her wrists with extra fabric hanging free from wrist to armpit. Black patent leather pumps completed her outfit, lifting her heels five inches off the ground. She still only came to my chin but it was the tallest she'd ever been. She'd curled her long brown hair and wore more make-up than ever, but it worked well with her racy outfit and made her even sexier.

I was speechless. My mouth silently opened and closed several times. She giggled.

"Good answer," she teased.

***

My best friend Alan works at one of the hottest spots in the city so I text him we were coming and he sneaked us in. We found a booth off the dance floor and got comfortable. I know the waitress thought we looked too young but she let it slide and we ordered three rounds of drinks up front and tipped her well.

"To life!" Julie exclaimed, raising her shot. I tapped her glass with mine and we downed it. She quickly grabbed the next one.

"To the future!" she toasted. Tap. Down.

"To hot sweaty nights dancing!" she roared before I tossed my drink down. I gulped it and lifted my last shot to hers, then opened the hatch and threw it down too. I'd get a nice buzz in the next few minutes but Julie, with her tiny body-weight, was about to get seriously smashed.

Julie loves to dance. I did my best to keep up but no way I am in the same kind of shape she is. Lucky for me the club was filling up fast and Julie just stayed on the dance floor by herself when I told her I needed a break. The crowd closed around and swallowed her. Last thing I saw were the faces of males and females lighting up when they laid eyes on her. She was a sexy tease for both genders.

I caught my breath and waited to stop sweating.

The crowd parted slightly and I saw a glimpse of Jules dancing with a good looking, conservatively dressed, thirty-something couple. The husband danced with Julie and then spun her to face the wife who danced a bit and then turned her back to face the husband. All of them were laughing and having a blast. The front of Julie's dress would gap so much I was sure the couple caught flashes of my wife's big perky tits.

Julie backed into the woman and ground her ass against the woman's groin. The husband leaned in to kiss his wife. Julie was sandwiched in the middle and wrapped her arms around the man pulling him in even tighter. The wife broke off and kissed all along Julie's nape and I saw my wife's eyes roll back in her head.

I was about to leave my stool and intervene when the waitress returned with our next round. By the time she unloaded and I paid her, my wife and her two new friends were once again swallowed by the crowd.

If I left our table someone would snatch it so I stayed put. Forty-five minutes later a somewhat guilty looking Julie made her way back to our table.

I shouted over the music, "Don't worry about it, Honey, I'm happy to see you so happy."

She gave me a weak smile and downed her first shot.

"I saw you with your new friends," I yelled. Her eyes grew big.

"You saw me? And you're not angry?"

I shook my head. "No, Baby, why should I be? You're just having fun."

She studied my face.

She cupped her hand to my ear. "You mean you saw us dancing."

"Yes," I hollered. "What else could I mean?"

Julie shook her head and took a shot, then crunched ice from her drink.

"I went back to their booth with them," she said. "I let them feel my tits. The wife, Michelle, slipped her hand up under my dress and a finger around my panties. She rubbed my clit and it felt amazing. They invited me up to their penthouse but I told them I was here with you so they invited you too."

"She did what? Are you serious or are you fucking with me?"

Julie downed her second shot.

"Serious. I'm sorry, Honey. It happened so fast and I'm pretty buzzed. Let's just dance some more and forget about them."

She grabbed my wrist and pulled me to the dance floor.

It was exciting that an attractive older woman felt-up my wife but I didn't like that I wasn't there when it happened. I got over my annoyance pretty quick though; that woman was hot.

I noticed some guys checking out our table so I told Julie to keep dancing as I went and shooed them away. When I got back to her the couple had reappeared and all three were dancing again. Julie was laughing hard and having fun. When she saw me she waved me over and above the roar of the music introduced me to Michelle and Tom.

Michelle put her arm around Julie's shoulders.

"Your girl is gorgeous!" she yelled. "Just look at her; she's an angel!"

I nodded that I understood how she felt. Julie looked sheepish and shy and buried her face in Michelle's neck. We all laughed. Michelle lifted Julie's face by the chin and gazed into her eyes.

"You are one of the prettiest women on the planet," she said earnestly. "And I know my husband agrees." Michelle leaned down and kissed Julie softly on the mouth. When Julie didn't pull away, Michelle got more aggressive and an instant later both women slipped their tongues into the other's mouth and kissed hot and passionately. My dick jumped in my pants. Michelle was very pretty with just a touch of Asian about her and her long jet-black hair fell around both their faces. I looked at Tom but he was as mesmerized as me. In fact, many on the dance floor watched that kiss and some even cheered and hollered.

Both women opened their eyes slowly, clearly dazed by the intensity of their kiss. Tom held Michelle's hand, I took Julie's.

"We are going upstairs," Tom stated. No one argued.

We left the club and after a minute Julie let go of my hand and took Michelle's and both women walked ahead. Michelle's tan, knee-length dress hugged her curves and accentuated her gorgeous ass. Tom saw me ogling his wife's ass but only smiled.

They told the truth when they said penthouse. The elevator took us to the very top floor. The insides were palatial. I asked Tom what he did for a living and he replied, "Make a lot of people a lot of money." I left it alone.

Michelle stepped to the control panel for the sunken indoor Jacuzzi and activated the jets. A soft hum filled the suite and bubbles rose to the surface. All eyes were on her as she reached behind and lowered the zipper of her dress. Julie looked at me for guidance but I was unsure what to do. Michelle was sexy and I wanted to see more of her but I was worried about my wife. Michelle dropped her bra and panties. Her breasts were much smaller than Julie's but fit her frame perfectly. Her pussy lips were partially hidden behind a closely trimmed curtain of jet-black pubic hair. I looked at Julie and her eyes were glued to Michelle. When Michelle smiled at Julie, my wife looked at me and slowly moved a hand to the zipper of her dress. If I was going to say something to stop all this, now was the time. Julie was giving me a window.

But I said nothing.

Julie took my tacit response as acceptance and slowly drew down the zipper under her arm. She stepped from her dress.

I'm not just a proud and loving husband boasting; Julie has a world-class body. Jacob may have ulterior motives but his business-eye is accurate; Julie would make them both a lot of money. I glanced at Michelle and Tom and they were frozen, seemingly hypnotized by my sexy wife. Julie stood in her panties and black stiletto pumps and every one of us just stared and stared. Michelle spoke first.

"Angel, take those panties off. You don't want to put on wet clothes later."

Julie looked at me again but I was still too stunned by what was happening to speak. I loved that Michelle and Tom could not rip their eyes off my wife but I didn't want Tom touching her. Julie reached down and off came the shoes and down came the panties. Michelle stepped up to her and they kissed again and this time Michelle gently cupped Julie's right breast. I heard my wife gasp and saw her body melt. Michelle teased Julie's puffy nipple with a thumb.

"You are so young, so beautiful," Michelle said. She bent her head and kissed a nipple.

Julie and Michelle began making out passionately. I felt my penis swell. The ladies explored each other with hands and lips and tongue. When Michelle slipped a hand down to my wife's pussy, I heard Julie gasp. She quickly returned the favor and I gawked as both women fingered each other as they kissed.

Tom joined me with a tray of drinks. Carefully handing me mine, he sat two drinks down for the girls and took his own. I sipped. It tasted odd and I asked him why and he replied he likes to use certain rare Russian vodka. I believed him and thought no more about it.

Michelle led Julie by the hand into the large tub. They sat right next to each other and I imagined what their hands were doing under the concealing foam. Tom took a few sips and then set his drink down. Hands went to tie and then shirt and then pants and I stood there and did nothing other than gulp my drink as he undressed. As his undershirt hit the floor both women turned to watch him finish and I was surprised at the great shape he was in.

Tom made quick work of his belt. Shoes went flying. Pants came down and off. Tom straightened and hooked thumbs and now down came boxers too. His penis was a long and wide tube of pink flesh topped with a fat head. I only caught a glimpse of it because I looked quickly at Julie. She was gazing directly at her third dick and gulping her drink. Tom floated over next to Michelle.

Everyone turned to me. Great. I swallowed the last of my drink and kept my back to the Jacuzzi as I undressed. As luck would have it, probably because I was feeling a lot of anxiety, my penis was especially small and shrunken. That always happened when I was nervous. I pulled on it twice discreetly before I turned around and entered the water, but it didn't help much. Tom and Michelle shared a knowing look.

The tub was built for two so four of us made it a snug fit. Under water our legs bumped frequently. Everyone enjoyed their drink and we all chatted about what we did and how we all met our spouse. After a while Tom noticed I was the only without a drink so he rose from the water to make me another. Julie's gaze went right to his cock again and Michelle's gaze went right to Julie.

Tom or Michelle must have played with it underwater because when he emerged he was much bigger and looked pretty long and big around. Julie stared right at it. Tom kept his pubes trimmed close just like his wife. Tom moved to the bar and the rest of us went back to our conversation. Tom returned and handed me another tumbler like the first and this one had a strange after-taste too. I was now buzzed enough I didn't worry about it. He slipped back into the tub. Soon everyone was talking a hundred miles an hour.

At the first lull in the conversation, Michelle floated closer to Julie and held her face as she kissed her again. I was surprised by the passion of Julie's return kiss and saw arms moving underwater.

"God that's beautiful," Tom whispered. I agreed. He appeared to be playing with his dick under the foam so I played with mine but I must have still been too nervous because absolutely nothing happened to it; not even an inkling of the beginning of a swell. Still, my hand felt great so I continued.

After some time Michelle moved in even closer to Julie and helped lift my wife's petite body up onto the edge of the Jacuzzi. My wife's nipples were swollen from all the attention Michelle had given them. Julie clearly loved everyone looking at her. Michelle parted my wife's knees and moved up between them, suctioning her mouth on Julie's pussy. Julie cried out and her eyes closed and her head fell back. She held Michelle's head in place. Tom and I moaned at the same time. Then he lifted himself onto the edge too. His cock was big and hard as he worked it with his hand. Mine was still small and soft so I stayed underwater. His balls bounced as he jerked it.

When Julie opened her eyes she first looked at me, then down at Michelle, and then over at Tom. Her gaze riveted to his meat and stayed there as Michelle tongue-tortured Julie's pussy lips and clit. My wife climaxed while staring at Tom's cock.

Michelle rose up and kissed Julie, teasing her sensitive nipples yet again, and then running her hands all over Julie's tone body. She nudged Julie back from the edge and laid her stretched out on her back. Michelle left the water and offered Julie a small, hard nipple to suck. Tom slid around and kissed Julie's feet and then her ankles and I knew I needed to say something but, again, I didn't. Everything was happening so fast and Julie was so captivated. If I stopped it now I'd embarrass her and Tom and Michelle. I pictured how awkward getting dressed would be for us all. On a deeper level I sensed Julie wanted me to let this happen. I was frightened but I admitted I'd been sucked into the tornado too.

Tom brought his hands up to Julie's legs as Michelle alternately fed her each breast. Julie moaned deeply as Tom kissed each leg, slowly working his way higher. Michelle moved lower, taking Julie's extremely sensitive nipples into her hot mouth and my wife tangled her fingers in Michelle's hair and shoved her tit deeper. Tom kissed Julie's inner thigh.

My head was foggy. Tom was getting too close and I was about to call him back when Julie reached her other hand down and found the back of his head and guided his mouth right to her pussy. I've never before heard a groan like that escape her throat and it froze me in my tracks. My words of caution died in my throat. My wife had decided to allow another man to eat her. The sight was intensely exciting and I reached for my soft penis and tugged but still, nothing happened. The threesome held their places for a long time.

Eventually Tom moved. He knelt beside my wife and Michelle did the same on the other side. Both of them feasted on my sweetheart like she was a zebra carcass, electrifying her with mind-boggling pleasure. It only took a moment before Julie was out of her mind, writhing and gasping and moaning as Tom and Michelle drove her wild with hands and mouths and lips and tongue.

Somehow through it all Julie remembered me.

"Wait," she cried. "Where's my husband? Where's David?"

"I'm here, Baby," I answered, leaving the tub and moving to her side.

"Are you okay?"

"I'm fine, Honey."

She glanced down at my soft penis and frustration crossed her face for the second time tonight. *Not again,* her eyes seemed to say.

"I need you to fuck me, Baby," she pleaded. "*Please!*"

I jerked my dick faster, desperate to get hard, but nothing happened at all. Not even a whimper. Tom and Michelle stopped long enough to look at each other and smile. I saw Tom's large pink tongue swirl around my wife's clitoris before his mouth once more fastened to her slit. Julie groaned like a demon had just possessed her and her hips began to undulate against Tom's mouth.

Michelle pulled back and gave her husband a kiss on the cheek and then moved over and sat on the deck next to me. Tom ran his hands over Julie's big tits and slipped an erect nipple into his mouth. He never stayed at one place very long, his mouth and hands and tongue exploring my wife's fit young body. He moved to her feet again and sucked her toes and licked her insoles. Julie was arching her back and working her hips, a knotted ball of desire and frustration. Tom grasp her ankles and spread her open and I saw her pink slit part and gleam. Tom once again began a slow march of kisses up her legs, alternating from one to the other. Julie tried to grab his head to force his mouth back to her pussy but he caught her wrists and pinned them to the deck.

Michelle reached into my lap and squeezed my aching balls. I grabbed her wrist. She gave me a smile that would melt iron.

"I'll be good," she purred. "Seems only fair since Julie is having all the fun."

I released her wrist and checked on my wife. Tom moved his knees between her legs and kissed and licked high on her thighs. His cock was so hard it looked ready to burst. He still held Julie's wrists and moved to pin them up next to her ears, then leaned down and kissed her. His cock brushed dangerously close to her opening and I told him he wasn't allowed to fuck her. He pulled back to kiss her stomach and breasts, removing his dick from the danger zone.

At the sound of my voice, Julie looked at me and Michelle. She saw Michelle's hand in my lap and saw that I was still as soft as taffy. She groaned and kicked her heels in frustration.

Tom leaned up to kiss Julie on the mouth again. This time he rested the weight of his big tool on her lower abdomen and I saw her jump at the contact. Her hips instinctively curled up to capture the penetration she craved. I felt a rush of excitement that she wanted it. She dug her heels in and lifted her entire pelvis off the ground.

"Poor thing," Michelle intoned. "Look how badly she needs it. As a woman, I can tell you the ache she's feeling is excruciating. Right now she feels an empty hollowness that eats at her. She's a woman. She needs to be filled."

Totally in control, Tom lifted his hips high enough for Julie to see his engorged and rampant cock. She growled in desperation. Tom dipped his hips and sawed the bottom of his prick against Julie's clit.

Julie turned her helpless eyes to me.

"Pleeeeeese," she whined.

"Baby, no," I begged. "We're married, Honey. This has gone too far. We shouldn't be doing this."

A milky drop of pre-cum leaked from Tom's slit and dripped onto Julie's light pubic hair.

Michelle spoke, her voice low and strained. "But you are doing it, and deep down you like it. Any other man would have stormed out long ago, or never come upstairs with us, yet you are here, watching others touch your gorgeous wife. That tells me all I need to know about you, David."

I fixed my gaze on her. Was she right? Refusing their invitation never entered my mind. Julie's hips rose and fell in time with Tom's.

"Look at my husband's beautiful manhood. Does yours compare? Imagine what incredible differences Julie will feel. She's so young. Has she known only you?"

I nodded my head. I was looking at Tom's hard veiny cock. Honestly, I doubted Julie could take it. She was so tight on me. His wouldn't fit. How could I even imagine such a thing? Was I actually considering allowing this?

"From the first moment on the dance floor, my husband and I knew you would hand over your wife. Your face as she danced with us told us everything. You want it as badly as she but you're afraid; you're afraid of losing her to him, of destroying your marriage, you're afraid of your own animal desires."

Tom worked his knees forward so he loomed over my wife. Julie's chest was heaving as she gazed into his eyes. I saw fear there, but it was mixed with longing and lust. Julie's inner pussy lips were so engorged they protruded.

My wife looked at me with sadness and runaway desire. I was confused until I realized she hoped I would understand, but she had surrendered.

Somehow, Tom knew and released her wrists and Julie used one hand to pull his mouth down to hers and the other to grasp his throbbing shaft and lubricate the head with her own wetness, rubbing it all around her opening. Her legs rose up and surrounded his waist; her heels pulled his hips forward.

I saw his cock-head mash and then split her inner labia. A burst of panic seized me as I registered he wasn't wearing a condom. Michelle read my face and proceeded to throw salt in my wound.

"Isn't it perfect?" she purred. "He will truly be inside her, his skin touching hers. From this moment on you are no longer the only man to have fucked your wife."

Julie breathed hard and squirmed. One more adjustment and Tom was perfectly lined up and my wife lifted her hips and pushed herself onto his first inch. Both groaned loudly from the penetration and Tom leaned his body weight down, driving another few inches deep. She was dripping wet and ready but several strokes were needed before Tom was fully seated inside her. Thick Tom forced Julie to accommodate him.

Another man was fucking my wife.

Another man was fucking my wife!

My sweet Jules had her strong legs wrapped around him and pulled him deep on every thrust. He grunted and groaned and she gasped and wailed. Her lips stretched into a tight O-ring around him, air-tight and bright pink. Surrounding flesh sank in each time he drove his shaft home and her pussy volcanoes with each withdrawal. This man drove my sweet wife insane with his hard cock. He bit her neck and sucked her nipples and she screamed and twisted and urged him on.

"Fuck! You reach so far inside me... I'm gonna cum so fast. Don't stop!"

Tom had no intention of stopping. His wife Michelle was pretty and sexy but Julie was a Youthful Goddess and urged him on, encouraging him to fuck her brains out.

Tom turned into an animal, his muscles flexing as he drove his meaty stake again and again into my Julie. Every time I thought he might be hurting her Julie grabbed his ass or his shoulders and told him to fuck her harder. Michelle had a wild look in her eyes as she leaned in and blurted, "She's going to orgasm!" She loved watching her husband seduce other women. His power over them was her power over them.

"Oh fuck!" Julie exclaimed. "Oh fuck oh fuck oh fuck! Oh, Christ AAAAAAAA!'

Tom's hips were like a piston as Julie climaxed, her hot body wrapped like a fist around Tom's big spear. She pulled her own hair and wailed again and then gripped his shoulders and urged him on. I saw Julie have the longest and most powerful orgasm of her life and I was crushed by the knowledge that it was not me or my penis that gave it to her.

Michelle moved around behind me. She placed her hands on my shoulders and whispered hoarsely into my ear.

"You know what this makes you, right? Have you heard the word they have for husbands like you? I bet you have. God! That's so hot! How must you feel at this moment? My husband is taking your wife. Look at his big cock plunging in and out of her. That's your woman and you're allowing it!"

Michelle couldn't take anymore and began fingering herself. She climaxed fast and hard as we both watched Tom conquer Julie. I was insanely aroused. I couldn't believe I was still soft as butter, but my heart was pounding. My penis and balls felt so wound-up with sexual tension I thought I would explode if only I could get hard. I tugged a few times but sensed an erection was impossible.

"If your dick was hard would you try to fuck me?" Michelle teased. I turned from the action to look at her. "You haven't even asked me to suck it," she continued. "I suspected we'd be able to seduce you both but I'm surprised at how far you've allowed this to go. You don't even care that you've gotten nothing. I would have fucked you just so my husband could fuck your wife but this way's better. Believe me, when you think back on this night you'll be glad it played out this way. You'll have no illusions about what happened. You didn't allow him to have her so you could have me; you just gave her up for free. Ask yourself why you did that."

I turned back to Tom and Julie. They were locked in a passionate embrace; Tom on top, driving his cock repeatedly into Julie's womb, Julie's arms and legs wrapped as far around his big body as she could get them. Her hips lifted to meet his every time. Another orgasm began to rise in her.

"Tom!" she cried. "Oh Tom, you're going to make me cum again! Oh fucking Jesus! Ooooooh Myyyyy Gaaaaawd! AAAAAAAAaaaa!" Julie's body jerked and convulsed beneath his. Her screams were incoherent gibberish. Tom never slowed or broke rhythm and her climax lasted almost a minute. He sent my wife skyrocketing to someplace way above earth. I'll never give her what Tom can and that hurts, yet also fuels a deep and humiliating excitement I do not understand.

Tom wasn't finished. He positioned himself on his knees and aimed Julie's legs straight up. He bent them back and her cunt splayed obscenely. He plunged his entire length and girth balls deep on every thrust. She seemed so vulnerable and unprotected. She whimpered and mewled as he pounded her. She was at his mercy and as her husband I did nothing to protect her. Shame boiled up inside me but I also felt the first stirrings of my long missing erection.

At this moment she belonged to him, not me, and he was free to do with her as he willed but more importantly, *she wanted him to,* and God help me but that really turned me on. My wife gave herself completely to another man. Tom's long fat cock plumbed the depths of her and soon my wife was ready to cum again.

Julie was quietly sobbing. I heard her whispering, "So good, so good, so good," and I knew her tears were tears of release and satisfaction.

Michelle saw my soft, partial erection and knelt behind me. She reached around and began to stroke as Tom bore down on Julie. I heard the little squeaks Julie makes as her orgasm begins to take hold.

"Is she on birth-control?" Michelle rasped.

I shook my head. She gasped and her hand on my penis sped up.

"Perfect! Do you use condoms with your own wife?" Her voice held a quality of disbelief, like someone stumbling across a chest full of gold coins.

I shook my head. "I always pull out."

Her hand felt so good. I was less than half hard but already cum boiled up. I knew exactly why she was asking and shame rose again. I felt so depraved for wanting to see it.

Michelle and Tom shared a look and she gave him a quick nod. Understanding passed between them. Tom skewered me with a hard stare. Tom cupped Julie's ass and began to slam her pussy hard. Julie loved being fucked like this. Tom was not some boy the same age as she. Tom was a man and Julie felt the difference in every way. Tom fucked her with strong and sure strokes, leaving his head deeply buried and pressed against her cervix half a heartbeat before pulling almost all the way out and doing it again.

This time her orgasm started from deep inside her uterus. Fatigued muscles and jangled nerves pulsed back to life as the hot electricity of climax spread from her womb outward, building slowly, wave upon wave as her entire body slowly clenched and tightened. Tom felt her pussy squeeze him. Extra effort was required as he pulled his shaft in and out. He felt like he was fucking honey. Although soaked to the point she was actually dripping, Julie's young and inexperienced pussy had never held a cock as big as his. She gripped him like a fist as she drove towards yet another earth-shaking orgasm. Tom sawed his cock as his sac drew up against his body and his hips moved faster and faster.

My mind reeled. Fear and regret drove me to speak but a deeply buried desire kept my mouth shut. Part of me rebelled against the inevitable and screamed at me to do something, to stop this insanity, but the simple truth was I *wanted* to see it happen.

"Here it comes," Michelle hissed, her hand stroking me even faster. "I know his signs. Watch."

She needn't have bothered; my eyes could look nowhere else. Tom fucking my breathtaking wife was the only thing that mattered to me at all.

Julie came before him, arching her back so hard I worried she'd break it. Her scream of release shattered the room and rang in my ears. Tom drew in all the air in the suite and held his breath but Julie was slammed by the next wave and screamed again, her fingers clawing the floor and her legs pointing straight up at the vaulted ceiling, shaking uncontrollably. My wife burst into tears as Tom's cock drove her on and on. She threw her head side to side and sobbed and wailed and pounded the rug with her tiny fists.

Tom gripped her at the waist and held her body a foot off the floor. His long pole was a blur as he hammered her until he sank it one last time and roared like a lion, throwing his head back and his hips forward and pumping a white-hot jet of his potent sperm deep inside my wife. Balls deep, I knew he must have entered into her uterus. Instinct told me she'd completely opened up on the inside. She'd dilated to accommodate his penetration, granting him access to her most fertile chamber. I knew he'd just launched two hundred million children inside her and that perverted knowledge finally gave me the semblance of an erection I'd been waiting for all night.

"Milk it!" he bellowed. "Fuck! Your cunt is milking my cock!"

Now it was Tom's turn to throw his head side to side as Julie's greedy little married cunt fluttered and sucked every drop from his big testicles. As her climax continued, her lower abs rose and fell, sucking cum from him. His back arched again and his hips pumped again and he released another blast and then another, pumping sporadically for a moment, jerking and jumping, as Julie teased out another bolt of semen. Tom's seed began to leak from the seal of Julie's labia around his shaft.

"Fucking Hell!" he cried and filled her with another jet and another. His ass flexed and clenched as he tried to squeeze every single seed that he could get out and into her. At last he laid her on the floor and held himself above her on muscular and trembling arms, both of them were gasping for air.

My eyes were welded to the place where their bodies merged. It was excruciating to see the way her lips so lovingly clung to his big shaft and his milky sperm dripping from her most intimate opening. If I end up condemned to Hell, such will be my view for all eternity.

Tom had taken my sweet wife in a way she'd never experienced. The sight was pure agony and I fed off of it. I'd never seen anything so erotic. I hated it and loved it. I ground the truth of what just happened into my mind like salt into a wound. Michelle pumped her hand even faster and although I was still a long way from hard, I shot my load all over the floor and her hand. My head spun as I kept myself from falling. She dropped my penis and wiped her hand on the rug.

Tom rested his big body on Julie. His cock remained stiff enough to stay inside her, acting as a plug, holding his seed within. I could not pull my eyes away from the meshing of their genitalia. They kissed slowly and tenderly. Tom kissed her soft neck and her large breasts too. Julie basked in the moment, looking as if asleep; eyes closed, a slight smile on her lips.

I had no idea what to say or do.

Michelle rose and moved beside them. She softly kissed Julie and Julie opened her eyes. Her smile broadened and the two women kissed again, sharing a mutual understanding and appreciation of sex with Tom. After a moment, Michelle indicated me with a jerk of her head. Julie's eyes met mine.

I thought perhaps as reality rushed in she'd be crushed by guilt and shame, and I did see a hint of both, but then she smiled and extended her hand. I took it, kissing her fingers. Michelle nudged Tom and he lifted himself off my wife, slowly withdrawing his slithering buried snake. He retained quite a lot of stiffness and her pussy clung to him still, sorry to see him go. Their mixed juices dripped from his head to the floor.

Julie slipped a finger down to check how big a mess she was and raised the digit to her lips. She tasted Tom's semen.

Tom and Michelle stepped back into the swirling waters of the hot-tub, giving us a moment of relative privacy. Tom sat on the edge and Michelle floated between his legs and began cleaning his impressive shank with her mouth.

Julie and I just stared at each other. What does one say at a time like that?

Julie decided to lighten the moment.

"Oops," she shrugged, trying to look cute and succeeding.

I ran my eyes over her smooth skin. When I got to her belly-button I considered what had just been deposited beneath it. Julie wasn't a virgin but she had been an ejaculate virgin. That was gone now, given to another man. That fact sizzled my brain but I had no idea what to do about it. The concept was too hot to touch. I was unable to ponder what it meant. The one thing I knew with certainty was I felt a deep, rolling arousal.

Julie's eyes held only a tiny hint of guilt. She had taken what she wanted.

"Oops?" I repeated. I felt a wild madness dancing all around me. I started giggling which built into a laugh. "What the fucking hell just happened?"

"I have no idea, Baby, but it was fucking hot. Are you mad at me?" Julie's eye had the madness too.

I shook my head. "No, I feel like I should be but how many opportunities did I have to stop everything?"

She rolled over so her face was close to mine. "Honey," she whispered, breathy exhilaration in her voice, "He came *inside* me. No man has ever done that before, not even you, and the first man that does is a total stranger? I feel so naughty and slutty. Do you think he's made me pregnant?"

Her pragmatic and innocently spoken words squeezed my guts. I hid my reaction because deep down, it turned me on too, and that embarrassed me. What kind of man was I? How could I not only accept this but welcome it and find it so erotic and exciting? Conflict rocked me.

"I don't know, Sweetheart," I said. "We'll buy a test on the way home. It's killing me that he's inside you right now. The idea is like a hot penny blistering my brain tissue. I can't stand it that another man got to have you like that and I haven't. Why is it hot that he came inside you but I can't?"

Her eyes softened. She touched my face tenderly. "He got to *because* he's not you, David. I couldn't act responsible with him without ruining it, so I just let myself be carried away. What a memory we've made."

She leaned in and kissed my lips. She sat up a little more. "David, I came so hard on him. You saw; can you ever remember me cumming like that? I didn't even know I *could* have orgasms that hard. I know this must be killing you. I am happy you didn't do anything with Michelle."

I was starting to feel uncomfortable. I knew Michelle and Tom were listening. I needed time alone with my wife to talk about all of this. Julie was always so much better at putting her feelings into words. I glanced over at Michelle and Tom. "Honey, how do we slip away and head home?"

Julie followed my eyes and then looked back at me, guilt in her eyes.

"Do we have to, Sweetheart? Can we stay a while? They're so beautiful and sexy and hip. They're like a power-couple. I want us to be like them some day. Can we hang out for a bit?"

Every time I looked at Tom, my face flushed. He had taken my woman. He one-upped me. He'd totally conquered her and he'd conquered the other woman in the room too. In our little group of four, I was at the bottom of the masculine power totem-pole.

Michelle lovingly licked his big spongy cock and caressed his fat balls like he was a King. Tom's eyes were closed and his head back, allowing Michelle to service him. I had to admit I wanted to run. I was embarrassed to feel this apprehensive and intimidated. I decided to play it cool.

"Okay Honey," I told Julie, relenting.

She gave me a big, heart-felt kiss and asked me to help her up because her legs were weak. Cum ran down an inner-thighs.

Tom and Michelle saw us approaching the Jacuzzi with the intent to join them and they both smiled broadly and made room for us. Julie surprised me by cutting in front so she could sit next to him, leaving me the spot next to Michelle.

"Fantastic!" Michelle gushed. "I was sure you two would bolt for the door. What a night! Tom, get your lazy butt up and make us all more drinks."

Tom rose and headed for the bar. I caught Julie scrutinizing his body as he walked. I marveled at the hidden power of sex. Tom was in charge. I was subordinate to him because he'd had my woman but I'd not had his. Now that I knew how Julie felt about the idea, I was not likely to ever have Michelle. Julie slipped next to Michelle and boldly kissed her mouth.

"You are so pretty," Julie said. Michelle looked surprised.

"And you are the sweetest thing ever. I called you an angel earlier and I was right."

"Thank you. Where did you buy those shoes you were wearing with your dress?"

At this point I bailed on their conversation. Julie can talk about shoes for hours. Instead, I turned my attention inward.

My eyes stared at the passing foam but my mind was watching Tom fuck Julie. The reality was too hot for me to touch directly and I thought on it in quick snippets and flashes of pornographic video. I'd witnessed a side of Julie I never suspected. What else had she not shared with me? When did she decide to fuck him? Probably downstairs while they were all dancing.

I glanced at the girls but they were talking a hundred miles an hour. I checked on Tom and studied his naked body, his penis still not fully deflated. He was a stud, I gave him that. Under the water I felt my penis. I was back to my previous shriveled state. What the hell? The water was hot but my dick and balls were more retracted than I could remember. I was glad the suds hid me. Tom walked back to the tub with another tray of drinks. He passed them out and slid in between Michelle and my wife. The three of them covered one side of the tub while I sat on the other.

With Tom back the girls ended their clothes conversation. Michelle sipped her drink and laid her head of his hairy chest. Julie surprised me by snuggling up under his arm and gazing up at his face. Tom began a story of drunken revelry while on a business trip to London and Julie sat enthralled. I saw Michelle slip a hand down and guessed she was playing with Tom's dick.

Tom followed that story with another. He and Michele traveled the world doing many interesting and intriguing things. Julie's face showed how smitten she was. I also noted that Tom and Michelle knew exactly the effect they were having on my young wife. I gulped my bitter drink, finishing it off.

The movement of Michelle's arm under the water was obvious now. Tom finished his drink too and rose to sit on the lip of the tub. Michelle had him nearly erect and he looked like a sea-serpent with the water cascading and running in rivulets off him. Julie was caught by surprise as a big, fat, hard cock was suddenly mere inches from her face. Tom towered up from his lap, the hot water making his huge balls hang way down. My wife confidently reached up and wrapped her fingers around his shaft. She knew she had permission.

Julie remembered I was sitting across from her and paddled over to me, her eyes filled with a question she never asked. She kissed me on the cheek and paddled back, once again taking Tom's erection in her hand. Michelle lowered her mouth and sucked one of Tom's balls. Tom sipped his drink, staring at me. Not until Julie closed her hot mouth over the crown of his cock-head did he take his eyes from mine and look down at the women in his lap.

I watched my wife. She was infatuated with Tom. She was a porn-star as she worked his big dick, using her hands and lips and tongue to pull every moan and gasp from him. She forced as many inches into her mouth and down her throat as she could, making herself gag but holding still and waiting for it to pass. Inch by inch she opened her throat and accepted more of his meat. There was no way she could deep-throat him; he was too long and too thick. I think she imagined all the other girls before her that sucked that cock and she competed with them. She wanted him to remember her above all others.

I'd never seen this view of Julie sucking dick. She'd only sucked mine and I either saw the top of her head of curtains of hanging hair. She looked so sexy and naughty with a hard cock in her mouth. I wondered if she would finish him with her hand like she always does me.

Tom's face slowly became a mask of amazement. My wife took more of his dick down her throat than anyone before her and now he held the edge of the Jacuzzi and enjoyed it. He knew he wouldn't last long and he didn't. Gently resting a hand on the back of my wife's head, he gasped a lungful of air and growled and then grunted as he filled Julie's mouth with cum. She gulped and swallowed and he gave her more, gritting his teeth and moaning. I was both crushed and thrilled she'd done it.

Tom lay back on the floor with his legs still in the water from the knee down. Michelle moved to Julie and kissed her, slipping a tongue into her mouth to taste her husband in there. They kissed passionately for several minutes until Michelle broke off the kissing and rose to the tub's edge pulling my wife's mouth in to her cunt. I reached for my shrunken penis. Julie hesitated only a split-second before taking a pussy into her mouth for the first time in her life.

Girl-on-girl has never done much for me but I can tell you watching Julie tongue-fuck Michelle was one of the hottest things I'd ever seen. Julie has no desire for women but my wife licked and sucked and fingered until Michelle had an earth-moving orgasm. When she came down from it she lay next to her husband.

Julie floated over to me, beaming with pride.

She nudged me from the water to the edge so I boosted myself up and onto the lip. She moved between my legs and sucked my shriveled peanut into her hot mouth and it felt amazing but after several minutes I was still was a small as a radish. I didn't understand. Nothing like this ever happened to me before. Was I secretly intimidated by Tom's big cock? Julie gave an exasperated sigh and gave up.

"Two out of three's not bad," she joked. "Are you okay?"

"Yeah, I don't know what's wrong. He must be tired."

"What's a horny girl to do?" she teased, bobbing in the suds.

"Trade me places," I said. Her eyebrows went up.

"Okay," she said. "Are you sure, Honey?" I gave her a quick nod, trying not to think about what I was doing.

As she rose from the water I was once again, just as I always am, struck by her ridiculous sexiness. Her globular, perky tits bounced around and the water ran down her flat and tone stomach. She turned away for a moment to step onto the seat and her long, dark hair, plastered against her strong back, sent water running down and over her small firm bubble-butt. I have never wished harder for an erection than I did at that instant.

She sat and it was my turn to drift over and spread her knees. Her pussy lips were still engorged. I moved closer, noting the inner lips protruded slightly. I leaned in to kiss them, but she reached down and with a hand on my forehead, stopped me.

"Baby," she crooned. "Are you sure about this? Remember, he's, um, still in me. I feel him dripping."

"I'll try it and see," I answered. "If it's disgusting I'll stop."

Lust blazed in her eyes. I think it turned her on that I wanted her pussy so much I was willing to break such a taboo. She used both hands to pull my head in.

I was tentative at first, afraid I would stick my tongue into a puddle of Tom's jizz, but it wasn't like that at all. She was extra slippery and salty and there was a slight bitter aftertaste, but nothing like the well of poison I was expecting. From the moment my tongue made contact with her tender lips my wife began moaning in sexual bliss. I was soft and gentle and soon forgot the evidence of another man as my wife quickly climbed to orgasmic heights. When she came she was squeezing my head between her muscular thighs and grinding her clit against my tongue, which was as far inside her as I could get it.

I floated away and glanced at the others and was surprised and embarrassed to discover them both sitting up and watching me. Tom's eyes held a wild look. Eating Julie after he'd filled her was a powerful ego boost for him, like he was also conquering or dominating me.

The timer on the Jacuzzi clicked off.

"How about a group-shower to wash off the chlorine?" Michelle suggested.

Tom and Julie agreed and all four of us headed for the master bedroom and the giant walk-in shower. As I exited the hot tub I tried to act cool but all three of them cast quick glances at my wilted equipment. Tom's dick was swinging all over the place.

We helped each other wash and shampoo and both women worked Tom's cock into a frothy lather. We rinsed and moved to the bedroom and Tom and Michelle gave us their robes. Michelle tied a towel around her waist electing to go topless and Tom slipped on some white boxers and made us all another drink.

Conversation flowed from work to sports to movies. They were an engaging couple and easy to like and so I wasn't surprised when, less than an hour later, Julie set her drink down and walked to Tom, knelt beside his chair and fished his cock out through the opening in his underwear. I saw my wife begin a slow, leisurely, and loving blowjob. My nuts tightened like they'd done a million times already tonight but once again I did not get hard.

Michelle came and sat next to me on the bed as Tom caressed Julie's hair, stroking her head and murmuring sweet affectionate things to her. Tom's cell rang on the end-table next to him and he answered and began a back-and-forth conversation with someone about an investment, but Julie never stopped. She got him to lift his hips as she slipped off his boxers, and then slowly licked his big balls and growing shaft. She opened his legs wider so she could get under and behind his massive scrotum, a move he seemed to enjoy very much.

"Look how she adores him," Michelle sighed. "I understand completely."

Michelle rested her chin on my shoulder and we watched Julie together. Tom ended the call and set the phone down but allowed Julie to continue.

"Your wife loves being his pet. See how she yearns to please? Tom has collected several women over the years. I find his sexuality intoxicating, and I love watching him seduce other women, but especially so when there's a husband present. I think you'd be shocked to discover how many men are willing to share their wives with him. Sometimes they do it for a chance with me but more often they just want to see their wives fucked."

I know what she was saying really held a deep meaning for her, but I was seriously distracted by her perfect tits. Hers were smaller than Julie's but they had a beautiful shape. The nipples rested high on each globe.

"Do you want him to fuck your wife again?"

I met her eyes. She already knew the answer but wanted to hear me say it. Julie and Tom heard and both turned to face me. Julie held Tom's fully erect penis straight up, anticipating my response. Up to now, Julie had impulsively led us far afield. This choice was laid at my feet. If I said yes, I was choosing to give my wife to him. I was handing Julie over to Tom. Julie sensed the difference and her eyes danced with excitement. She was ready for more and I was completely unavailable. In her hand was the cock she craved and I admitted I wanted to watch her again.

I looked straight into my wife's lovely eyes. "Yes."

Julie beamed. I'd made her very happy.

Tom stood, his hard cock wagging briefly, and took Julie by the hand. In two steps he was next to the bed and he took Michelle's hand too.

"I'm taking them to the guest bedroom where I can be alone with them. You've been drinking so I doubt you should drive. You are welcome to crash on the couch or dress and head downstairs to gamble or dance or whatever. When we've finished I'll have Julie text you."

For a moment Julie looked as if she wanted to say something but her mouth opened and closed silently. I felt slapped. My first instinct was to tell him to fuck off and grab Julie's hand and leave but the look in her eyes stopped me. She wanted Tom to fuck her again so badly her eyes were pleading with me. I knew if I made a scene she'd come away with me, and I was grateful for that, but it would just be home to a cold bed and frustrated sleep; there was no way I was getting hard again tonight. I felt it. I knew it. Everybody in the room knew it. I rejected going home alone, or even going downstairs. I needed to stay as close to Julie as possible.

"The couch," I said at last.

Before my wife could lean over and give me a kiss, Tom turned and pulled them to the other bedroom. I caught a last glimpse of Julie quickly dropping to her knees and opening her mouth as he closed and locked the door.

If watching another man fuck my wife was difficult, not watching but listening was a thousand times worse. After thirty minutes I was tied in a knot and after thirty more I was in a fetal position covering my ears. It sounded to me like my wife was in a state of continuous orgasm and Tom was no doubt filling her womb with gallons of hot sperm.

I was sure Michelle and Tom made Julie the focus of their desire and based on her screams of pleasure, poor Jules was happy to take it. After another hour of relentless fucking, I covered my head with a couch cushion. I was insanely desperately to cum and played with my dick constantly but absolutely nothing happened. My whole body was super-charged and ready to explode but I had no outlet whatsoever.

Eventually their room fell silent. I heard the girls occasionally giggle and Tom's deep rumbling laughter once but no further sex sounds. I thought I was in the clear. I turned on the television and waited for Julie to reappear. But she didn't and much later when I heard her utter a deep and throaty moan I knew they were back at it again. I grabbed more cushions and buried my head.

***

This is exactly how I awoke hours later. I glanced at the room and was surprised to discover the door slightly ajar. I crept over and peeked into the room.

All three slept soundly on the bed, piled like nude puppies in a tangle of arms and legs. I risked entering and circled the bed soundlessly. Tom was in the middle with Julie's head on his hip and his dick less than an inch from her mouth. Michelle lay across his legs, curled into a ball. I felt strange seeing him slumber like this; he was human after all.

Someone must have risen for a drink of water or to check on me and returned to bed without closing the door. Each of them breathed deeply, no doubt finally exhausted. I moved around to Julie's side and studied her naked form. Christ, she was lovely. With every deep breath she took, her pussy leaked milky cum, her lips bright pink and swollen. Her nipples, also bright pink and swollen, were still erect and seemingly eager for more.

I thought about waking her and sneaking us out but worried she would refuse. After everything we'd shared, I was sure she would not skulk away in the middle of the night.

Good manners might seem odd at a time like this but I knew how Jules would feel and I would feel it too. Tom and Michelle had done nothing to us against our will. I had no right to be rude.

I kissed Julie's hip and she stirred slightly, moving her face towards Tom's cock until it made contact with her face, which tickled and she brought a hand up to scratch her chin. When she set her hand back down it was directly on Tom's shaft and her fingers instinctively closed around him like a microphone. A small smile curled the corners of her mouth.

I chanced a few cell phone pictures without sound or flash, just to capture the moment, and then returned to the living room couch, silently closing the door behind me. I was sure I would lie awake until Julie came for me but surprisingly I drifted off, awakening only when room service knocked on the front door with breakfast.

Rising first, Tom had ordered food for us all. We sat on the huge bed and ate and nobody mentioned the night before. We were old friends sharing a meal and chatting.

We all group-showered again but I took the longest. Then Julie and I dressed. Tom and Michelle remained naked. At the door Michelle gave us a wink and a smile. These people were insatiable.

Julie was quiet on the drive home and I attributed it to fatigue. Of course I was dying to know what happened behind closed doors but I wasn't going to pry it out of her. She'd talk when she was ready. I didn't want her thinking it bothered me more than it did.

Ready turned out to be about three hours later. Without a word she approached me while I was on the computer and took my hand, leading me to the bedroom. She slipped her sun dress off her shoulders so it fell in a pile at her feet. She wore nothing underneath. I started to ask questions but she placed a finger against my lips and sank to her knees. Her hot mouth felt wonderful

What followed were the most intensely sexual two hours of my life. For some reason I still was unable to get erect but Julie didn't care. Each time I reached for her she gently moved my hand away. She was focused on giving and did not want to be distracted by receiving. She loved my penis. She worshiped my penis. She caressed and adored my penis. She treated me so well and so unselfishly I began to wonder why.

It was two hours before the first inkling of an erection formed and when it did Julie got terribly excited. It took me another fifteen minutes or so to become almost fully erect but it felt amazing. My entire body ached with stored sexual tension. I reached for her again and now, distracted by my hard dick in her mouth, I slipped a finger inside her before she could stop me. I was astonished at the amount of sperm she contained. Tom had flooded her insides.

Julie slipped me from her mouth and straddled me and her neatly trimmed pussy engulfed my penis. She was so slippery with Tom's semen and her own juices I slid in without any resistance at all.

I knew I wouldn't last but Julie didn't care. In fact, she seemed especially eager for me to cum and as I felt myself get close and tried to pull out, she slammed her cunt down around me and ground her hips against mine. I exploded like a warhead, flopping around like a fish, pouring hours and hours of sexual frustration and desire like a fire-hose out of my dick. She didn't climax. She laid her little hard-body on top of mine, waiting for me to catch my breath.

Once I had I asked her, "What brought that on?"

She looked at me with soft eyes. "A couple of things," she said. "First, you just gave me the most amazing night of my life and I know it was difficult for you and at times really difficult for you. I wanted to say thank you for trusting me. I wanted to show you that in spite of all those things you watched me do last night, I still belong to you. I'm sure there were moments you doubted that."

She leaned back a little to see my face better and went on. "David, I have hidden so many thoughts and feelings from you and that is bad for us. I was afraid you'd judge me. I was afraid there was something wrong with me. I have such a sexual mind. At times I felt so dirty, buried under an avalanche of dark fantasies and yearnings. But I feel like last night set me free, or at least set us on the path to freedom. A year ago I would have been invisible to Tom and Michelle. The sweet things they said about me and to me make me want to shed tears of relief."

She stopped, waiting for my reaction. I told her I agreed with what she was saying and encouraged her to continue. Her face got very serious and intense.

"Second, I have something to confess and I'm not sure how you're going to take it. It's something I learned only this morning."

I nodded for her to go on, now suddenly very interested.

"At Tom and Michelle's suite, while you were finishing up in the shower, Tom walked me to the bar. He had something to show me."

Julie was so serious dread filled my belly.

"It was a small orange bottle. He showed me the label, Xanaphosphate, but it made no sense to me so I asked him what it was. He called it anti-Viagra he'd picked up in London; a few drops in a man's drink and he won't get an erection for hours. Tom gave it to you so he could have us girls to himself."

I was stunned. Then I was angry. Then I laughed. Loudly. Part of my brain was screaming at me to go back to angry, to threaten to kick Tom's ass or sue him. But instead I laughed. My reaction surprised Julie as much as it did me.

"Why are you laughing? I thought you'd be pissed."

"I think I'm so relieved to find out nothing is actually wrong with me or my dick!" I laughed again. "Holy shit! That fucking snake! He's a master at his craft. That was the ultimate cock-block."

"I can't believe you're not furious."

"I was for a second and I guess I should be, but why? What's the point? I don't like that he drugged me, but you said yourself last night kind of set us free. We both now have a big part of who we are out in the open. We're still in love, closer, even. Why get mad? He's a bastard for tricking me but look at what he gave us. Look how alive we feel."

"Oh my God you're amazing!" she said and hugged me tight.

***

The pregnancy test we bought needed a week after last coitus so we enjoyed a tense seven days. The day she took it we held our breath, only exhaling when the result showed negative. We fucked like animals right there in the bathroom. The reality of what we were testing for made us both insane with lust. Sometimes it was hard to imagine the encounter with Michelle and Tom really happened, but watching your wife urinate on a stick to see if she carried another man's baby sure made it real.

For the next six weeks Julie and I lived an amazing life; our intimacy was off the charts and we made love almost every night; during sex we talked dirty to each other about the things we'd done.

One Friday night I came home from work to discover Julie masturbating with a dildo about the size and shape of Tom. She was soaking wet. The toy gleamed. I wanted to strip and pounce on her but she told me no, sit and watch, I want only Tom tonight.

When she climaxed she shook the bedroom with her screams. I was hard as rock. After came back to earth she crawled next to me and held up the erect plastic cock next to my dick. He was larger in every way. Her face was coy as she told me to jack off into my hand. I came in less than two minutes and washed my load down the bathroom sink. My wife was becoming a master at this game.

The next morning Julie and I were on the patio under the misters enjoying a cup of coffee and the news. The scent of honeysuckle occasionally drifted by and the air held a hint of that brutal Vegas heat. I turned the page on my Kindle and realized she was staring at me and had been for a few minutes.

"I'm horny," she said. I reached for the sleep button and started to head for the bedroom.

She touched my hand. Her eyes were mischievous.

"No, I'm *horny*," she said again.

I sat back down. Understanding dawned. In all the hot-talk we'd shared over the past two months, never had we discussed how to make something similar happen again. The planets all aligned that night and it happened so easy and naturally. How do we make it happen again? My wife craved a cock other than mine and that was exciting and intimidating. I wondered if holding silicone Tom next to my penis last night was the finally straw for her. I know she longed for bigger.

I swallowed in a dry throat. "Let's shop for a new dress today and we can hit the club tonight. Good idea?"

"Not bad, but I have a better one." Damn her mischievous eyes.

She slid Jacob's business card across the table at me. I tried swallowing again but my throat just stuck closed. I coughed. My body temperature soared. Julie chuckled.

I lifted the card, turning it over in my hands.

"You've been thinking about him lately?" I asked.

"A lot. You know why."

Indeed I did. Jacob was even bigger than Tom.

"How do we do this?" I inquired.

She reached for her phone and began tapping out a text and then sat her phone down.

"What did you say?"

My wife tilted her face back to catch the morning sun. "I asked him what I could do to make the maximum amount of cash, and how much I would make doing it."

"Oh. Wow."

"Yeah."

After a minute of silence her phone chimed. She read his reply. She laughed. I waited. She showed me.

"For you? Porn. $5,000 daily."

Julie set her phone on the table. We regarded each other.

"No," I stated flatly. She laughed again.

"I know, Baby, that's too much even for me. I want a connection to the guy, not just some asshole with a big dick."

She keyed another text, speaking out loud as she typed; "Gross. What else do you have for me?"

He responded right away; "I sold your pics for top dollar so anything you want. Studio, tomorrow, one o'clock. No husband."

I felt my face burn. "That sucks," I said. "That's no fun for me. I'm a visual guy."

"Think of it as being on the other side of the bedroom door," she teased. "You know how to do it. Besides, it's a photography studio. I'll insist on lots of pictures to bring home."

I felt my penis stir. I was still bothered by her 'connection to a guy' comment. She feels a connection to Creepy Jacob? She must have read the look in my eyes.

"What's the matter, Honey? Have you changed your mind? Do you want me to behave? Shall I be a sensible wife?"

"No, but what connection can you have to Jacob? I don't understand why you like that guy. He's a pervert. He takes advantage of young girls."

She came around the table and sat on my lap.

"We owe him. You know that, right?"

I jerked my eyes up to hers. "What? Why?"

"Remember that day in the dressing room? The way he looked at me? That was the straw that broke the camel's back for me. I finally realized, after all those years of rejection, men wanted me, and not just ugly men but hot men, successful men, wealthy men with big cocks that could have any girl they wanted and yet had eyes only for me."

Oh.

She went on, "Because of him our conversation that night happened. Because of our conversation, we went out dancing. Because we went out our night with Tom happened, and here we are. Jacob is so sexy. I've seen him naked and he's seen me naked and that feels like intimacy to me, like we've already shared something. His cock looks bigger than Tom's and Tom's drove me insane. I can't begin to describe how intense it feels to have a man that large and that hard inside you. Jacob's body is in better shape too."

My penis was starting to stiffen and I knew she felt it against her leg.

"Jacob is sexier than Tom," she added. "Jacob exudes sex; the way he moves, his muscles, his hard ass, his eyes, his mind. Tom is handsome but had an arrogance and distance about him. Jacob is smitten by me. I can see it in his eyes; he adores me, lusts after me like crazy. He wants me badly."

She slipped a hand into my shorts and squeezed my erection.

"Honestly, Love, I think I know what he'll do to me. I see his caged passion and I recklessly want to set it free. I don't expect you to understand completely. I think it's more a woman thing; men see us and desire us and we want them to, some men anyway. I love being desired by men."

Her phone chimed again. She released my dick and left my lap. She read the message.

"No fucking way," she breathed. She read it again and lowered her phone. "Jacob says there's another choice. He didn't offer it because he was sure I wouldn't be interested. He says there's a king-size bed in a storeroom at the studio. He sometimes shoots live-feed sex shows for his online porn site. Members pay a fee and log-in to watch the performance. He'll give me five thousand dollars to fuck him live on the Internet."

My jaw almost hit the table.

"You're a visual guy," my wife reminded me. "At least you'll get to watch."

Julie replied she'd do it. Jacob was ecstatic. He asked for a week to advertise the event and a date set for next Saturday night at nine. The show started at ten but he wanted her there an hour early to go over logistics.

Julie set her phone on the table with trembling hands.

"Oh my God!" she squealed, kicking her feet. She picked her phone back up and fired off one last quick message and slapped her phone down again. I raised an eyebrow.

"I told him I've thought about him since that day in the dressing room. I said I loved how big he was. I told him I think he's sexy. I asked for a picture of his penis erect to whet my appetite all week."

She sat on her hands. I was uncomfortably hard. Her phone chimed. She lit the screen and pressed a few buttons. Her eyes narrowed and then grew wide.

"Holy shit!" she cried, laughing. She stared at the screen for another minute, absentmindedly touching her lips, scrutinizing the image. She handed the phone to me.

Jacob held his hard, thick, vein-laced cock with his fist at the base. His fingers did not meet on the other side. His large shaved ball sack rested on the chair between his legs. His shaft held space for at least two more fists above the first.

I was totally and completely intimidated. This was not a spontaneous event Julie and I got swept-up in and carried along by. This was premeditated, pre-calculated, intentional infidelity. My wife was going off to fuck another man without me. Our marriage felt incidental. The urge to tell her no was growing in me and it was fueled by her admission she felt a connection with him. True, I was hard, but I was frightened. I was jealous. I was insecure.

"What if I said no?" I blurted.

Julie's face froze but then softened. I saw understanding and empathy in her eyes. She stroked my hair. "Then I would cancel, Sweetheart."

She picked up her phone.

"Would you be angry? Would you hold it against me?"

"Not at all. I know our arrangement isn't fair to you so I'll take whatever you allow me. I don't want to hurt you, David."

She opened the text conversation.

"Don't," I said. "Not yet. Give me time to think about all this. It happened so fast."

"Okay, Honey, let me know what you want to do."

I stared at the table top but from the corner of my eye saw Julie ogle Jacob's photo again.

The subject did not come up again all day. That night Julie and I made love soft and slow. She is so incredibly beautiful; her soft hair surrounded her high cheek bones and full lips. Her big hazel eyes gazed up at me and I saw how much emotional damage I could do to her if she lost me. She made sure I knew she was mine.

***

The next day we puttered around the house and watched *Fight Club* in the evening. When the film ended Julie slipped her head under the blanket and sucked me until I shot down her throat. My powerful orgasm wiped me out and I silently thanked Tom for teaching her she had to do that.

She moved up and curled under my arm. Everything seemed fine, but I knew it wasn't. The air held expectation. I was being the petty, jealous husband and I knew it. I'd watched Tom repeatedly fuck her and fill her with cum. Why draw the line now? I felt small-minded and immature. She was genuinely being the bigger person and I hated that I couldn't be. Did I care about what she wanted? I was a selfish child. My neck burned. Better to hand her over to Jacob for one night and live with the consequences than go on like this. If next Saturday came and went without Julie meeting Jacob, I would feel like shit the rest of my life. I couldn't bear to be that guy. She would never say a word but I know her disappointment would be huge. I decided to say something before I turned coward again.

"Jules, Baby, you can go next Saturday." I couldn't even say his name.

Julie squealed and hugged me fiercely. She sat up and clapped her hands.

"Thank you so much, David. You don't need to worry, Honey, he won't steal me away from you." She kissed my lips.

By Tuesday I was anxious. By Thursday I was manic. Almost every night I had dreams of Jacob slow fucking my wife and instead of turning me on they made me sick.

Because I am a masochist, on Friday morning as we got ready for work I asked her to tell me more about how she felt about Jacob. I was desperate to try anything to make myself feel better and I thought if I knew her mind more clearly the fear would diminish.

"He's intense," she began. "He has intelligent eyes but listening to him talk in the studio that day confirmed he's smart. He's really handsome; like movie-star handsome. His bright blue eyes kill me. I know he's had a million girls but I don't care. That makes him even more attractive. Usually that's a turn-off but not with him. I love that he can have any girl he wants and he picks me."

Julie was drying off after her shower and I imagined her body in Jacob's arms. It hurt. I saw her dainty pussy lips, covered in neat and closely trimmed pubic hair, disappear into Jacob's ravenous mouth. I heard her cries of ecstasy as his tongue split her open and wormed deeper. She'd worked out harder after our encounter with Tom and Michelle and her body was now absolute perfection. Her big breasts naturally thrust out and up and I knew Jacob would devour the small puffy nipples that topped them. His hands would run up those strong, shapely legs and cup that firm, bubble butt.

Everywhere and every time he touched her, my wife would respond with soft moans filled with deep longing. Most men never know when their wives are hot for another man. They fool themselves into thinking it doesn't happen. I envied them. Not only did I know but I also knew in detail *why* she wanted him, and I'd seen the impressive cock he'd be using to fuck her. For the hundredth time in the last few days I thought again about calling it off and just living with the repercussions. Julie would get over it. I wouldn't but Julie would. I shook my head and returned to what she was saying.

"His body is so manly. I know I'm still a girl in many ways and my body shows that, like my nipples for example. Your body does too; your chest is almost hairless and you still have some baby-fat. Everything about Jacob's body screams adult male. He's a *Man*. Most of all I love his big, swinging dick. Holy fuck that thing makes me hot. It's like all his masculinity is concentrated into one object."

We finished dressing and said our goodbyes. At work I was a distracted mess and made several mistakes. I finally concentrated, pushing all thoughts of Julie and Jacob out of my head, and finished the day strong. As I left the office, Julie text me to meet her at *Georgina's*, one of our favorite Italian restaurants, for dinner.

As they showed us to our booth, almost every head turned to look at her. I was so proud she was with me. Growing up I never expected to land a girl like her. She wore a simple black and white knee-length dress with her hair pulled back into a pony-tail. She wore no make-up. None of that mattered. Her undeniable beauty was natural.

We were halfway through dessert when I noticed she was looking at me.

"What?"

She leaned in, speaking in hushed conspiratorial tones. "Tomorrow is the big day!"

Her face was lit with excitement, her eyes sparkled. "I was thinking," she continued. "We didn't have sex last night or the night before. I think we should skip sex tonight too. I will be practically virginal when Jacob gets his hands on me. There will be no trace of you to detect. I want you but just think how hot you'll be when I get home. You'll tear me apart!"

I smiled and agreed. Honestly, I wondered if I'd even get hard tonight. My anxiety was sky-high. We finished our meal and drove home separately.

My fears of impotence were unfounded. Julie came out of the bathroom wearing a sheer black baby-doll. She was freshly showered and ready for bed. I took one look at her and my penis swelled faster and harder than it ever had before. I remembered this outfit from Victoria's Secret but she'd not worn it since. She stood at the foot of the bed and turned slightly side to side.

"You like?" she teased.

"Like? Are you fucking kidding me? I love it! Baby, you look sexier every day!"

She grabbed the covers and yanked them back, revealing my hard on.

"Did I do that?" she asked.

I lunged for her but she jumped back out of reach.

"No touching," she reminded me. "If you're a good boy, I'll show you my surprise for Jacob. Do you promise to behave?"

I settled against the headboard. Julie leaned her back against the bedroom wall and spread her legs about shoulder width apart. My eyes ate her alive; that young ripe body, bursting with sexual vitality was too much to take. She kept her eyes glued to mine as she reached a hand to the little black bow that kept her panties tied to her hips. She pulled the ribbon and the triangle of black lace curled away. She untied the other side and the material fell forward, exposing her tiny bare mound.

She'd shaved herself utterly hairless. Her little bald mons gleamed at me, tight skin shiny and fresh. Hairless, I saw how small she really was. Tom may have been in Heaven but Jacob would lose his mind. Hot jealousy seared my guts. She'd done it for him. I'd mentioned it many times over the years but she said she never would, because only sluts did that.

She giggled and I realized I'd been staring. How many minutes just passed? I looked up and she laughed.

"Baby," I breathed, my voice carrying every ounce of desire I felt for her. "You are seriously the sexiest woman on earth."

Her chest heaved a little as she drew a deep breath. Her lips parted. "Go on," she croaked.

I closed my fingers around my hard penis and stroked. "You're strong and sleek body is flawless. Your sweet face is angelic. You possess not a drop of arrogance yet have every reason to be arrogant. You have a face graced by God and a body crafted by the Devil himself. Jacob will be crushed. Jacob is about to get hit by a train."

She lifted a hand and untied the bow at her shoulder. Half her baby-doll fell away exposing a firm breast and flat abs. Her left hand cupped the breast still covered and the right sought her naked clit. Her deep breathing increased.

"Tell me more. Tell me about Jacob. God, Baby, I want him so much. What will he be thinking and feeling when he sees me?"

It stung, I won't lie.

"First he'll just stop and stare at you, unable to believe his great fortune. He'll silently congratulate himself for taking a chance that day at the mall. He'll want to touch you immediately but he's a little older so he'll probably be able to restrain himself so he can drink you in and never forget that moment."

She pinched a nipple and rubbed her clit faster. I stroked faster too.

"The front of his pants will bulge. Aroused blood will flow and he'll balloon rapidly. His mind will scream at him to rip your clothes off and take you. I don't know how long he'll be able to hold out."

A small gasp escaped her. "Honey," she whined, "I'm so sorry. I want him. I need him inside me." Her exposed nipple twirled in a circle as she rubbed her bald pussy.

I continued. "When he sees you've shaved for him he will lose his mind. If he hasn't taken his cock out yet he will after that. You'll gaze at his monster, that cock you desire so much and your little pussy will gush in anticipation. He'll see the look in your eye and know he has you; you're hooked, he owns you."

Julie moaned hard and I knew I'd struck a nerve.

"He'll bend you over and bring the camera in close. Everyone on earth, including your husband, will watch as he stuffs your young pussy with more cock than it can take. He'll treat you like a slut on a live feed and you will climax harder than ever from shame as the whole world witnesses what a whore you are for big cock."

Julie cried out and fell back against the wall. Her legs shook hard as she came. She looked so fucking sexy I couldn't hold back and came as well, shooting cum on the bedspread.

Hours later she was sleeping soundly but I wasn't. I was erect again and gazing down at her, dreading tomorrow night. Julie still wore the baby-doll and I realized being married to her meant other men would forever be involved in our sex life. Part of me loved that, part of me hated it. My eyes rested on her hairless and perfectly smooth labia. How often had I wanted her to do that? I sighed. No way was I sleeping tonight. I left the bed and surfed online until sun up.

I was useless all day. I'm not even sure how we spent it. Julie laughed and asked me, "Aren't I the one supposed to be a nervous wreck?"

Yes, only she wasn't. She was excited and couldn't wait to be with him. I had an overpowering urge to constantly jack off but I resisted it. I knew I'd want her when she came home and probably more than once.

Eventually, it was time. She stepped out of the shower and dried and I noticed she had re-shaved her pussy. Her whole body was hairless from the head down. She threw on a light green sundress with nothing underneath and flat sandals. She pulled her hair back into a sensible pony-tail. She wore no make-up. We kissed once at the doorway to our bedroom and several more times in the driveway. I watched her drive away.

I was much too early, but I entered our office and opened Jacob's website anyway. Julie had very thoughtfully left a bucket of ice, tumbler, and a new bottle of my favorite Jack Daniels, *Honey,* by the monitor. She also left a small, hand-written note;

David, my love, trust me when I tell you how precious you are to me. I never imagined I'd enjoy a life where my darkest fantasies were not only accepted and encouraged, but made real. I love you. Remember those words tonight, "I love you" no matter what you see or hear.

Jules.

My hand trembled with anticipation as I finished. I didn't wait; I poured myself a drink now. Then another. I surfed everywhere, checking back on the site often. At nine forty-five a portrait shot of Julie's gorgeous made-up face filled the screen with a caption that read; *Tonight! J-Man fucks lovely Natasha!* A stop-watch counted down from fifteen minutes. I took another drink.

Time   slowed   down.

"Fuck!" I yelled, pushing back from my desk. I paced the room then sat back down. I stood and stripped nude and then returned to my seat.

Agonizing minutes later, the screen faded and an interior shot of the huge bed came up. Jacob, J-Man, faced the camera.

"Friends," he began. "You've all come to expect quality porn from me. Tonight I bring you something that will haunt you forever. Just looking at her will torture you the rest of your life, knowing she is out there, and she is not with you. You will never touch her, so I will touch her for you. Don't hate me."

He waved to someone off camera. Julie, Natasha for tonight, entered frame and sat next to him on the bed. I groaned out loud.

Julie wore the same sheer black teddy she'd worn for me last night. Matching lace gloves, panties, and five-inch black stilettos completed her attire. Her hair was curled and her make-up, especially around her eyes, was heavy and bold. Her lips gleamed dark red.

"Tell us about you, Natasha," J-Man said.

The camera zoomed in on my wife's face and I realized at least one other person was in the studio.

"Well," my wife began, "First I want to tell you that I'm married, and my husband David is watching tonight."

"Really? Wow! That must be tough for him."

"It really is. He loves me but I know sharing me with you is going to torment him. He'll agonize watching us."

"Then why are you here?"

Julie turned to face Jacob. "Because of you. You're gorgeous and sexy and I want you so badly. I masturbated to that picture of your big cock all week. I can't wait to give myself to you. My husband will just have to understand."

The camera panned down Julie's young firm body. Her tits almost burst the seams of her lingerie, her puffed up and swollen nipples strained against the mesh fabric, pink flesh poking through the tiny holes. My mind reeled. My wife had masturbated *all week* while looking at Jacob's cock.

My phone lit up and buzzed. Annoyed, I silenced it and pushed it aside.

"Will you stand and show us how beautiful you are?" J-Man asked.

"Whatever you want," Natasha replied.

My wife stood and slowly turned in a circle. I bit a knuckle. She was more vampish than I'd ever seen her but that sweet, innocent face let her pull it off without looking skanky.

"Okay," Jacob said to the camera. Chat is now on. Send us your requests. Make Natasha do anything you want."

A small dialog box popped up on my screen and my phone lit up again. Julie would do anything she was told? What the fuck? Irritated, I checked my phone to see who kept texting; two friends from work, Chuck and Pete, one text each. I opened and read them.

Chuck's went like this: *Dude! Is Julie with you right now? If she ain't, you've GOT to check this website.*

A link was thoughtfully provided.

Pete's was pretty much the same thing. At least two buddies from work were about to watch my wife get her brains fucked out. I answered them both stating Julie was next to me on the couch as we watched a movie and why were they asking. They both said check out the site anyway for a girl that looked EXACTLY like my wife. Pete added he now had jerk material for a year. Awesome.

When I turned my attention back to the screen, Jacob led Julie to the side of the bed. She moved to the center, reclining on her back. Jacob ran a light hand over her fresh and vibrant body. Her youthful vitality radiated. He gently tweaked a lace covered nipple.

From the headboard he produced a padded handcuff. My neck burned and my temperature rose. Dread filled me. My smiling wife placed a willing and delicate wrist inside and J-Man clicked it shut. He repeated the process on her other wrist and then moved to her feet, securing each ankle the same way. Julie's chest rose and fell as she tried to control her breathing. I could not tell if she were excited or scared.

J-Man stopped and disrobed. His underwear was a black G-string which bulged massively in every direction. He hooked his thumbs and those came down too and his lumbering tool flopped out.

A tight black leather cock-ring separated his equipment from his body and accentuated his lumbering size. As soon as my wife saw it she began to squirm and whimper. He was not yet half-hard and already coiled veins stood out under the skin. The head was big and the shaft behind it almost matched the crown in thickness. It looked like a bull's cock.

As big and menacing as it was, his testicles were worthy co-stars. Twice the size of mine, maybe more, two swollen plums nestled in a tight hairless bag of sensitive flesh. I caught myself staring and looked away, embarrassed, but quickly looked back. They were really something to see.

Jacob hefted his rod and aimed it at Julie. Her eyes were glued. From beneath the bed Jacob withdrew a large vibrator and clicked it on. A low hum came from my speakers. He ran it up Julie's left leg and then her right, causing her to squeal with laughter and tug at the cuffs that bound her. He did it again but this time slowed as he approached her pussy. Julie drew very still and bit her bottom lip.

For the next thirty minutes J-Man used that vibrator to drive Julie crazy. He brought her to the verge of orgasm multiple times and backed off. If it were me she'd be getting angry but for him she writhed around and attempted to capture his cock with her mouth whenever he brought it close to her face.

"This is for you guys," Jacob said to the camera. "Remember that super-hot bitch in high school? Remember the Head Cheerleader or the sexy girl on the swim team? Here she is, and I'm getting her back for all those times she forced you to play with your penis because she wore a mini skirt to school. I'm going to fuck the Prom Queen on your behalf."

Julie groaned with frustration but he was merciless and masterful. It dawned on me he read my wife better than I did; backing off when she was only seconds from climax. I watched him handle my woman better than me. When Julie was almost in tears from sexual frustration, he turned the vibrator off and slid it under the bed. My wife's chest rose and fell rapidly.

Jacob exited screen and reappeared carrying a chain dog leash and collar, which he attached to Julie's throat. He freed her hands and told her to free her ankles. He led her before the camera and ordered her to sit. The camera zoomed in.

My phone lit up.

From Pete; *you're lying. That's Julie. Send me a picture of her right now holding up two peace signs.*

Fuck. What to do? I had no options so I ignored him.

The camera zoomed on my wife's gorgeous face. Her cheeks were flush. Her hazel eyes wide open and fixated on Jacob's manhood. Her lips were parted. Her sexual arousal was obvious to every person watching. From off screen a large, red, and partially inflated dick-head entered the picture aimed right at her face. Julie reached for it with her mouth but Jacob yanked the chain and scolded her.

"I am in charge, Natasha. Say it."

"You are in charge, J-man."

"Open your mouth."

Julie looked right into the camera and I swear to you she was looking right at me. A slight smile curled the corners of her mouth. This was so much different than watching her with Tom. The camera was right on top of them. I saw every detail; the lips I'd kissed so many times, the tongue I'd felt dance with mine, her smooth flawless skin. Instinctively she reached for Jacob's cock again and he once more jerked her chain. She pouted.

Off camera I heard Jacob say, "Look how badly she wants it. A woman this gorgeous so needy for dick? Do you love it because it's big?"

Julie nodded her head.

Jacob looked into another camera. "How many want to see her suck my fat cock?" I watched the dialog box on my monitor as user name after user name told him to stick it in. I was sure Pete and Chuck chimed in too.

"Start here," Jacob ordered, pulling her mouth down to his balls. Julie dove in. Finally allowed to touch Jacob, she moaned as she licked the bumpy flesh of his scrotum. I reached for my penis.

Nothing happened. I tugged and pulled. Nothing. That familiar blank feeling smothered my erection. I grabbed the bottle of Honey and peered deep into the golden liquid. Tiny strands of clumpy black oil swirled. Son of a bitch, she'd dosed me. Tom must have sent her home with some. I yanked and jerked and watched her full red lips close on the opening at the tip of Jacob's big cock, but nothing; not even the hint of a hard-on.

With no recourse or release, I would have to watch as my sweet wife finally gave herself to the man she craved most.

She'd sabotaged me. She'd be home hours from now, just as this drug was wearing off, knowing I'd take out my accumulated frustration and desire on her, and that's exactly what she wanted. With no relief available she knew I'd suffer through every anguished minute of her complete submission to Jacob.

Julie pulled her lips back to reveal the tip of her tongue working his cum-slit. She closed them and her cheeks dented from the powerful suction she applied. Jacob moaned. My wife was trying to pull his cum up from his testicles.

The camera panned back to show us Julie masturbating as she sucked. Several viewers commented how hot and sexy she was but they loved how much she loved dick.

Julie nudged him deeper. The camera zoomed in. Her taut lips stretched as he fed her another inch and I saw her throat move as she swallowed saliva and relaxed. Another nudge and another fat inch. There was no way she could deep throat him; she'd failed on Tom and Jacob was bigger. But she was going to try. She maneuvered her head, trying different angles until she found one she liked, then another nudge and another inch. I knew guys all around the world were jerking hard dicks. Probably a lot of girls too.

Julie's eyes watered a bit and she swallowed again. Deep breath and an angle adjustment and two inches slipped deep quickly. Surprised, Jacob sucked air and hissed his intense pleasure.

"Fuck ME," he growled. Who's in charge, Jacob?

My wife opened the seal of her lips and took a breath around his thick shaft. Jacob dropped the forgotten leash, no longer interested in controlling this woman at all. Julie held his hips with both hands and forced his dick farther into the warm enveloping tube of her throat. Jacobs's arms hung at his sides and his head fell back. This was a spectacle of pure slutty determination. She rested a moment then withdrew an inch, only to steel herself and take back that inch plus two more.

Jacob had perhaps three inches of fat cock left and I'd changed my mind; my money was now on Julie.

My wife rose higher on her knees. She held her head at an odd angle, like a turtle trying to run. The dialog box was going crazy. Everyone was cheering her on and telling her how insanely hot she was. She gagged for a second and I worried we'd reached her limit but she pinched her own nipple to distract herself and opened her mouth as wide as she could.

In one smooth cock-swallowing motion, the last three inches of Jacob's schlong slid home. Julie's throat bulged and she held herself perfectly still, her nose pressed against his pubic bone and his huge cock buried in her gullet.

"Oh my fucking God, oh my fucking GOD!" Jacob gasped.

The dialog box stopped scrolling completely. Every single one of us leaned closer to the screen and jerked our dicks as fast as we could. Julie's young and innocent face was stuffed with an engorged and veiny phallus. It was a vulgar and depraved moment, shocking and scandalous. Soft as cotton, my penis nevertheless longed to explode. The immoral vision on the screen made me want to scream. I yanked my penis as fast and as hard as I could, almost crying from pure sexual frustration. Jealous flared. Why did he matter so much to her? I knew it was pointless but I jacked my penis anyway. Jacob had his entire impressive length buried in my wife's esophagus. She was pinned like a butterfly in a collection.

Much later it occurred to me that Julie had done more than masturbate with that big Tom-sized dildo. Clearly, in anticipation of this meeting with Jacob, she had practiced her oral skills too. My wife so desired to please this man she taught herself how to deep-throat a cock as big as his.

Holding his hips, my wife began to fuck her throat on Jacob's cock. Her spit drooled to the floor as Jacob's huge balls rested against her chin and then slowly pulled back, only to slide forward to her chin again. Each thrust went a little farther and soon Jacob was fucking the length of his prick into my wife's food pipe. I was especially turned on each time his big nuts pressed against her lips.

Julie's confidence soared. Each time his balls pressed her face; her tongue swirled out and licked them. Julie rubbed her clit furiously, thrilled by her newly acquired skill. When Jacob announced he was going to cum, Julie moaned "uh huh, uh huh, uh huh," until he pushed the length in, held it there, and pumped a phenomenal amount of hot liquid straight into her stomach. His orgasm left him weak and he slowly fell towards the bed as Julie vacuumed the last precious drops from his tool.

Julie stood and looked into the camera. She licked her lips. I felt her in my mind. She wiped a finger across her chin and licked the drop of cum she found and smiled, directly at me and only me. She took a step back and the cameraman widened the field to capture her whole body and brought everything into sharp focus.

My wife gathered the bottom of her teddy and lifted it over her head, her gorgeous firm breasts magnificently on display. Her puffy nipples were engorged, begging to be sucked. She untied her tiny black lace panties and drew them from between her tone thighs. She shook out her hair and gazed directly into the camera.

This time she looked not into my eyes but into the eyes of every person watching her. She peered into Chuck and Pete and every male and female audience member that paid the price of admission, and feeling thousands of pairs of eyes crawling her skin, she dropped her head back cupped both breasts and soaked it all in. She connected with all of them. We all felt it. From my speakers I heard her moan. This wasn't an orgasm but something different; her body shook and shivered, goose bumps rose. Behind her Jacob leaned up on one elbow to watch. Julie was on full, wanton, whorish display and loved it.

My phone lit and I read; Pete told me in spite of what I said, he knew it was Julie. He *knew* it. He promised to keep my secret safe. He said she was an unearthly beauty and any man would be proud to claim her as his own and although she was at that moment sucking another man's cock, she was still my wife and that made me one lucky mother-fucker. He told me he wouldn't judge us and wouldn't I enjoy having at least one other person that knew it was really her? I remembered Julie had mentioned on several occasions that Latin Pete was sexy and I don't know exactly why, but that tipped the scales. I text Pete back, swearing him to secrecy, but yes, we were watching my wife.

"I knew it!" he quickly replied. "Brother, whatever floats your boat; it's your marriage. I'm just thrilled to finally see her naked. This last year she has totally blossomed into a real beauty. All the guys at the office hate you."

As bizarre and twisted as it sounds, I *was* proud she was my wife.

I returned my attention to the screen while a tiny part of my brain wondered about meeting Pete at work Monday morning.

Natasha wore only her black stilettos. Jacob showed us her back and bent her at the waist. Her baby-smooth slit stared back at the camera. Jacob pulled her round ass cheeks apart and showed the world my wife's dripping wet cunt. Her subtle back muscles rolled smoothly under her skin. With his fingertips he pried her lips apart and we collectively looked inside my wife's vagina. His actions were crude and salacious and turned me on but they drove Julie truly crazy. Her right leg shook visibly from arousal.

Jacob slid two fingers in and withdrew them, showing the audience she was soaked. He placed one slick digit at her anal opening and before she could tell him no, sank to the first knuckle.

Julie exclaimed "Oh my GOD!" and Jacob chuckled.

"You seem surprised how good that felt," he said. "Something tells me your sweet young ass is virgin." He turned to the camera. "What do you think folks? Shall I take her anal virginity?"

The dialog box lit up, affirmative answers rapidly scrolling by. I felt my face burn. My wife squirmed as Jacob's finger probed her rectum. Her hand held his wrist, but only in reflex; she wasn't about to stop him. By the time he was buried to the third knuckle both her legs trembled and she moaned as he finger-fucked her butt.

All this play had an effect on Jacob. The cock-ring probably helped but just twenty minutes after a thunderous cum-swallowing orgasm, he was hard again. He stood behind her and reached around, sliding a hand up Julie's stomach to play with her breasts. His erection bumped her leg and her head snapped around to see it.

They turned to face each other and their eyes met. I saw something pass between them. All showmanship vanished.

Of all the moments I had witnessed between my wife and another man, this one hurt the most. Her face held a look of pure joyful desire. She glowed. Her eyes held glee knowing she and Jacob would soon be making love. I recognized the look because previously she'd only aimed it at me.

Even in five inch heels she did not reach Jacob's mouth as she stretched up to kiss him. He leaned down and they gazed into each other's eyes a long moment, smiling and happy. Their bodies touched and Jacob's long cock slid up between them and disappeared, pressed like a hot dog between two buns. They hugged and my wife laid her head on his chest and sighed. She was so happy to finally be in his arms.

For the first time I saw in his eyes what she did; he looked at her with intense desire but only half of it was sexual. He adored her. He thought her something extraordinary and special. Jacob had fallen in love with Julie. He didn't just want to fuck her. She wasn't just another pretty girl. He looked at her and saw the whole world. Julie was a woman he could marry and spend his life with. Julie had recognized his gaze. I suddenly felt very threatened.

He had everything she wanted in a man and he had more of it than me. They both knew how the other felt. As I watched my monitor, Julie softly took his hand and led him to bed. In moments their love-making would bond them together forever and I would witness it all. I was about to watch another man take my wife from me. I had no doubt. I saw in Julie's sparkling hazel eyes that she likewise adored Jacob.

Julie knelt on the bed and they kissed again. She unsnapped the cock-ring and tossed it aside. Jacob removed her shoes and joined her on the bed, lying side by side, stroking her hair and softly kissing my wife.

Jacob gently pushed her onto her back and leaned over her. His eyes traveled her breath-taking beauty from nose to toes. He looked so happy. Julie did too. He began kissing her lips then moved down, kissing her breasts and nipples. The cameraman followed his mouth, zooming in as Jacob's tongue snaked out and teased her soft areola until they grew taut and erect. He then sucked them firmly, closing his lips and denting his cheeks.

My wife reached down and curled her fingers around his steely erection. With two light but urgent tugs she maneuvered him between her legs. She could wait no longer. He was on his knees with his fleshy spear curving gently up from his hips. My wife's hand looked so small wrapped around him.

"I've wanted you from the moment I saw you," she told him. "I couldn't believe a man like you even noticed a girl like me. But you did, and not just notice. You talked to me. You flirted with me. I couldn't believe it was happening. I saw in your eyes how much you wanted me. I would have given you anything you asked for, done anything you told me to do."

My wife's confession crushed me.

Her legs slid up his outer thighs until her ankles crossed behind his lower back. They gazed intensely into each other's eyes. I saw Julie falling in love with Jacob more each passing second.

"You're the most beautiful man I've ever seen," she breathed. "Even in movies. I've never wanted someone so much in all my life."

"You're the beautiful one," he asserted. "You may be the most gorgeous woman on earth. You are this age's Aphrodite. I haven't thought about anyone else since I saw you. You're married and I told myself to respect that but my heart leaped when I got your text. I want you so badly."

My wife shivered in pleasure at his words. They both looked down when she rubbed the large head of his cock around her opening, wetting it for penetration. The cameraman was right there. It killed me the way her labia clung to his flesh. Every part of her seemed to yearn for him. Other cameras recorded the action too but I was glued to the close-up. Julie's bald pussy looked so delicious and inviting and I envied Jacob about to claim it.

"Imagine how beautiful our babies would be," Julie told him. I heard them kissing again as Julie eased him forward. His rod dwarfed her pussy and he was hard as stone. The tip touched. She pulled him on. Her outer labia flowered followed by her delicate inner lips. His head was enveloped and smothered. When he flexed his hips, skin from all around her vagina pulled in. He pushed farther in and held still. Her skin slowly and gently slid back along his shaft. He was sinking into her half an inch at a time, allowing her to adjust and accept him. Julie groaned.

"Oh my God it's happening. I can't believe it. Baby, you are really here, with me, in me. You're so big! It's overwhelming. I'm gonna cum so fast. Oh shit! Oh shit! OOOOOhhhh mmyyyyy Goddddddd!"

Jacob pumped his dick with short strokes but Julie's first orgasm caught him by surprise. My wife lifted her head and their foreheads touched as she climaxed gazing deeply into his eyes. She was gushing juices and his cock was dripping wet. Her poor cunt already looked stretched to tearing.

Jacob gave her a long kiss as he sank his remaining inches home. My wife cried out, her voice cracking with pleasure and satisfaction and desire. She welcomed him, releasing a hunger she had carried for so long. At last she had him inside. He belonged to her. She had won, defeating all the other girls, capturing his attention and then his affection and soon his seed. He pulled out and slid home again and both twisted and gasped at the exquisite pleasure of their bodies merging.

Jacob adjusted his knees and pulled Julie closer and then pushed his cock all the way in. My wife flinched for a moment like he'd hurt her but then grabbed his thighs and pulled. Her legs were as wide open as she could get them. The cameraman must have been lying on the ground next to the bed because the angle showed Julie's pussy forced into an obscenely large O shape to accommodate his girth. Her stretched lips were white and formed a tight seal around his intruding shaft. A second later his hips blocked our view and only his massive shaved scrotum remained outside her body. My phone lit.

"Dude," Pete text, "He owns that pussy. How is this not killing you?"

I text back, "Are you fucking crazy, Dumbass? This IS killing me."

Pete replied, "I don't know how you're doing it. Let's grab lunch Monday. I want to hear ALL the details."

I knew on Monday Pete would also ask how he could have a shot with my wife. I hoped this wasn't the start of something ugly.

Back on the monitor Julie and Jacob were making love. Jacob's hips rose and fell in smooth tender waves and my wife writhed beneath him. They kissed constantly, affectionately, touching faces and hair and murmuring sweet things. If I hadn't been drugged again I'd be hard as diamond and jacking off. Julie had been right. She wanted me hard when she got home and I would have spent my seed in a voyeuristic orgy.

He cupped his hands under her ass and lifted, causing her legs to fall even farther apart and exposing her cunt in a splayed and lewd way. His fat prick sawed in and out, soon driving my wife into another intense climax.

Minutes ticked off. Jacob was every bit the stud I'd assumed he'd be with unheard of staying power. Poor Julie became a fleshy rag-doll, exhausted from several more orgasms and Jacob's relentless attention. I faced a harsh reality knowing I'd never, ever fuck Julie the way he was fucking her. If she was still mine after all this she'd have to come to me for something other than sex like this.

I had no idea how long they'd been fucking when Jacob rolled her onto her back and pressed his body down on hers. My phone lit and Pete text, "Here it comes!" and of course he was right; Jacob began his long climb to ejaculation and Pete and I both knew exactly where it would be going. Pete was smart enough to avoid teasing me about Julie having Jacob's baby, but I knew he was thinking it. Another man was about to fill my wife with his sperm and I would witness the moment with a good friend. I was humiliated.

Julie's legs rested on Jacob's shoulders as he drove his massive cock in and out of her. It was such a position of total submission and surrender that it stabbed a jealous dagger into my heart. He leaned forward, bending her legs back over her body, pinning her under his body and forcing her to take what he gave her. When he exploded he rammed his huge spear far up inside her and his large nuts lifted again and again, clenching and pumping as he squeezed out every drop of cum he had to give her. Jacob bellowed like a bull and Julie cried out, so pleased she had captured the sperm of the man she most desired.

The cameraman set the camera down and moved to the side, breaking down lighting.

Jacob stayed inside her a long time. After they'd caught their breath they nuzzled and kissed. I heard Jacob ask Julie to marry him. I stopped breathing. Mother Fucker. Julie laughed, her voice sounding like wind-chimes. When he didn't laugh too she realized he'd been serious and she laughed again. I wondered if they thought the camera was off.

"Why not?" he asked. "I love you. I know you feel it too."

Julie got serious. She glanced nervously at the camera once before speaking to him.

"That's true; I do love you, or something that sure feels like love to a young girl. But I'm with David. I'll always be with David."

"But we both feel it." he implored. "The love we just made proves it. I know you felt that connection too. I want you and only you and I want you to want only me."

"I do want you, Jacob, but I want David too. I'm young. I know men will enter my life and I'm going to want some of them too. With David I can have them but I know you'd never allow it. That's how my life was before. I'm not going back. That's just not who I am. David understands this and I'm lucky he thinks it's sexy. I'm sorry. I hope you understand. You can still have me. We can still be together, sometimes. But I'm married to David and it's going to stay that way."

Jacob rolled off her and onto his back. Julie sat up to look at him.

"I'm sorry," she said again.

Jacob glanced at the camera and his eyes narrowed. Understanding dawned and he smiled and raised his voice.

"Hello!" he said, waving.

He found a fixed camera overhead and continued. He told us taking her anal virginity would need to wait for another show and he'd let us know when, but for now this show was over. He wanted alone time with this world-class beauty. He pressed a button. As he turned his back on the camera and returned to the bed and my resting wife, the screen went back to the website logo.

***

Julie came home three hours later. I heard her car pull up and met her in the living room. She obviously had fucked Jacob again, possible more than once. I tried to help with her bag but she pushed my hand away and dropped to her knees and I knew this would be our pattern; Julie will fuck other men and come home to me ready to be reclaimed. I was already naked but soft and drugged yet she dove in and thirty minutes later had me fully erect. I wanted her pussy, not her mouth and bent her over the couch. Cum dripped from her unfaithful slit but I didn't care and slammed my penis balls deep with little effort. I was so wound up I came fast and hard, spraying her inside and adding my load to the ocean she already carried.

Later she told me Jacob had filled her two more times before she left him to come home, angry fucking her for rejecting his offer of marriage. She confessed she liked it best when he treated her a little rough. I assured her Jacob would be rough-fucking her from now on. Later that night I tried to take her ass but she stopped me.

"David, I'm so sorry, I told Jacob he could be the first. He promised his viewers and I want to honor that, but mostly I just want everyone to watch. That will be hot." I tried to get a little aggressive with her and she stopped me again.

"Honey, leave the rough sex to my lovers. Be my sweet loving husband. It's not your style anyway." She turned her back and made me spoon her.

I pouted until I remembered Pete. I told her what happened.

"Holy shit!" she exclaimed. "Pete from your work?"

I nodded.

Her eyes narrowed and she gave me a sexy, sultry look.

"He's the cute Latino guy, right?"

"Yes."

"Find out how big he is," she taunted. "I have to make up for lost time."

End.

Visit my blog; MyEroticBunny.tumblr.com

Get a FREE Cuckold/Vixen Story!
Join My Mailing List
http://eepurl.com/cTvA7P

Printed in Great Britain
by Amazon